A SIGNIFICANT EXPERIENCE

GWYN GRIFFIN

A SIGNIFICANT

EXPERIENCE

HOLT, RINEHART AND WINSTON

NEW YORK   CHICAGO   SAN FRANCISCO

Designer: Ernst Reichl
83283–0513
Printed in the United States of America

"One of the most ardent pursuits of man is finding excuses to persecute other people."

—Laurie Lee

A SIGNIFICANT EXPERIENCE

*S*UMMER—full Egyptian summer—curved its bright bowl of shining speckless blue over the great barracks which lay embedded in the dusty sprawling city, a huge cancerous red sore in the body of a laughing beggar. The sun, blazing out of the noonday sky, struck back in a pale glare of light from the white parade ground, reflecting heat waves which shimmered an aqueous haze over the hard surface. At one side of the square a squad of drill instructors, all sergeants, was going through its paces under the harsh barks and yelps of the chief drillmaster, a brigade sergeant-major of cavalry; they turned, stamped, wheeled as one man —a pale khaki ballet mimicking in stylized dance the formal eighteenth-century movements of war.

From the third-story window of his empty classroom Major Seligman watched them for a moment, fascinated as ever by their robotlike precision, and then, turning back to the sand table, he began to arrange the counters for this evening's exercise. He limped carefully round the table, aware that his leg was hurting him more than usual, the iron brace under his cherry-colored trousers itching and rubbing below the knee. Tanks on the forward slopes where they masked the fire of their own batteries—he would see the doctor this evening, or perhaps even after lunch if he was available—"A" Company trapped between a mine-field, green counters, and an exposed ridge—though probably he would only be given those pills again and they hardly helped at all, particularly at night—two platoons of "B" Company pinned down by enfilading fire from the right. Enemy armor, red counters, swinging round to the left in an attempt to outflank the entire position. That was sufficient to start with. On the blackboard he wrote: *What would you do if (a) You commanded the "I" tanks or (b) "A" Company or (c) Forward platoon "B" Company?*

"I know what *I'd* do, all right!" he muttered to himself as he put down the chalk and dusted his fingers. "I'd get the hell out of it—and double quick, too!" But this evening, when the cadets crowded round the table studying the layout, that was the one solution which none of them would dare suggest; they knew well enough that they could always achieve good marks by saying they would attack. They were all sand-table heroes. Not that Seligman believed them when they immolated their hypothetical platoons in this way, but he had to pretend to. Continual pretences on both sides; a rather nauseating game of make-believe, in which the class simulated fervent courage and self-sacrifice over the colored counters in order to satisfy their instructors that despite a lack of more formal qualifications they were fit for officers' commissions. But, "God preserve me from ever having to go into action with any of my lot!" Lutwyche, one of the company commanders, had said contemptuously.

Seligman had agreed. It was difficult to feel any liking for the cadets, far too many of whom were rendered servile by their probationary status and the rigid discipline of the training school. Their protestations of heroism were a price they were expected to pay, but the coin was false.

With a last glance at the sand table the Major picked up his cap and stick and left the room. This section of the great barracks was drowned in the heat-still silence of noon, and as he limped down the long corridors his uneven footsteps echoed hollowly from the worn floors. An Egyptian cleaner in shabby blue, swabbing disinfectant over the bug-ridden boards, paused to let him pass, and when he emerged onto the square a couple of cadets issuing from another door-way froze into rigid attention and saluted with the precision of mechanical toys.

Heat, dust, and the great multi-windowed walls of the old red-painted, vermin-infested barracks towering up on every side—a thousand men lived, ate, worked, and slept here, the great majority between the ages of twenty-five and thirty, in conditions at once claustro-phobic, tense, unreal, and fearful. Death hung in the air—bright, hot, brutal, and very open. Death was taught and talked about and feigned continually, in mock-ups and exercises and the panting, twisting rou-tine of unarmed combat, judo, bayonet-and-gun butt. From this place many would be sent to face death. Many had already done so—Seligman had, and now, walking slowly across a second smaller square to the officers' mess, he was thankful that he could not be called upon to do so again. It meant that he, at least, need not pretend to any enthusiasm at the prospect.

The officers' mess was a long two-storied building, low in comparison to the towering six stories of the surrounding barracks, and set in a small formal gar-den where canna lilies and geraniums grew stiffly, spaced in geometrical beds amongst the white gravel. The rooms inside were cool and high-ceilinged, with big dark armchairs and tables scattered with ash trays and out-of-date illustrated papers. A great sepia photograph of Kitchener in the uniform of Sirdar of the Egyptian Army, looming above two crossed sabres on one wall, stared arrogantly through an archway at the inevitable colored portrait of the King above the bar. Of the two, Major Seligman preferred the Kitchener photograph, for at least it was the only one; but George VI, sometimes alone, sometimes with wife and children, was ubiquitous, that blank, blue-eyed stare above the massively gilded and decorated collar of the full-dress uniform met one in offices, classrooms, stores, and passages. George VI, *Rex et Imperator,* the reigning Sovereign, Britannic Majesty, titular Commander in Chief—the man for whom, in a theory that was largely accepted as mythical but must nonetheless never be openly questioned, the thousand men in the barracks were sworn to fight and die.

As Seligman entered the bar two captains emerged, saluting him as they passed with the distinctive bent-wrist action of the Guards. In this place no one ever stopped saluting; but then saluting was a fetish with the Guards, and all the officers were either from the Brigade or the cavalry, for only élite regiments were expected to supply instructors for the training school.

There were two Guardsmen already in the bar when the Major entered: Captain Lutwyche of "E" Company—a badly built angular man with long blond hair, horn-rimmed spectacles, and a small pouting mouth which was never still—and one of his platoon commanders, a dark, hot-faced young lieutenant named Hood. They were discussing their company as Seligman limped to the bar, and they remained unaware of his presence until he had eased himself, sighing, onto one of the tall, leather-topped stools. ". . . that's what he'd get, of course, if this was Sandhurst. But as it isn't—Good morning, sir! I didn't hear you come in. What can I offer you?"

"Hello, Lutwyche. Well, a beer, I suppose." Seligman took his cigarette case from his pocket and at once young Hood pulled out his lighter. The junior Guards officers made a point of being particularly deferential to higher ranks in the cavalry, but it was a deference which was understood to conceal an aristocratic superiority, a sort of *noblesse oblige* which should never be taken at more than its face value. "By the way, Hood, this morning's report showed five of your platoon put on light duty, or so the Adjutant says. What have you been doing to them?"

Hood grinned. "Assault Course mostly, sir. They hate it."

"I can't say I blame them."

"Good thing. Toughens them up."

"Not if they have to be put on light duty afterward. Do they really hurt themselves?"

Hood shrugged. "Some do—occasionally. It's not supposed to be a fun fair, after all. And half the time it's their own bloody fault; they don't think. Take yesterday, for instance, going over the wall. They have to do it in threes, of course. That's all right, if all three are much the same weight, but they never sort themselves out like that. Yesterday, White and Cobden, each of whom weighs over two hundred pounds, I should think, got hold of Van der Haar as third man. So Cobden heaves him up to White, who grabs him, and of course Van der Haar just flies over White's head and the whole thing's a shambles. They just don't use any bloody intelligence."

The Major took a long drink of beer and sighed. "That's why Van der Haar's on light duty then?"

Lutwyche said coldly, "He's malingering. There's nothing wrong with him that the doctor can find, but he says his back hurts. Actually it's because the company's on an all-night exercise tonight and he doesn't like night exercises; he'd rather go to bed."

Seligman shook his head. "My good Lutwyche, no one malingers here; they daren't. They know perfectly well that as far as they're concerned even a suspicion of malingering is one of the most deadly sins."

"Van der Haar doesn't know, or more probably doesn't care. He's discovered that if you go to the M.I. room and see old Cross . . . And listen, sir"—the tall Captain's face flushed angrily—"I was there this morning myself to—to see what had happened. Van der Haar was lying on the examination table on his stomach reading an American comic. Cross was in the dispensary with the door open. When I came in Van der Haar pretended not to see me. I waited a minute and then said, "You get up and stand to attention when an officer comes into the room." Cross heard me, I suppose, and shouted to Van der Haar 'You stay where you are till I've looked at you!' "

"What did he do?"

"That's exactly what *he* said, 'What do I do now?' and started giggling."

Seligman laughed. "But what *should* he do? I'm not a Regular like you two. I don't know these intricate niceties. *You* tell *me*."

Lutwyche looked offended for a moment. "He should get up, of course, sir. I'm his company commander."

"But he's in the doctor's inspection room and lying down on the doctor's orders."

"That makes no difference, I assure you. In correct regimental practice I'm his sole commander, his owner. He must always obey me before anyone else, except of senior rank. And even then there are circumstances in which, regimentally speaking . . ."

Hood cut in hotly. "It's not only that! That's typical behavior, what the Captain's just said—but he's like that all the time. He doesn't know anything, and when he makes mistakes he just giggles. He—just because he's been sent here for special reasons and has never been in the ranks—he thinks it doesn't matter! If this was Sandhurst he'd get a sharp dozen from his cadet officer, in fact, he'd have had them weeks ago. That's just what we were saying, sir, when you came in. If this was Sandhurst . . ."

"What if this was Sandhurst?" asked a cold voice from the doorway, and Exelfield, the Staff Major, entered. He was a tall man, impeccably dressed in Lancer uniform—boots, spurs, glinting buttons, and the big silver death's-head badges of his regiment on cap and collar—a pale-haired, pale-eyed man with a long scar across the left side of his face. Though only a comparatively junior major, Exelfield commanded almost as much respect from his brother officers at the training school as the Colonel Commandant himself. The Guards officers deferred to him because he was an immensely rich man from their own background. They knew that his choice of a lancer regiment was due solely to his passion for horses—he was a fine rider, a steeplechaser of courage and ability—and that otherwise he would have been one of them. The same considerations won the approval of his cavalry colleagues who, even though they were all mechanized, liked to forget their tanks and armored cars and remember the days of charges, sabres, and silver trumpets. What was more, Exelfield was ubiquitous; he placed the widest possible interpretation upon the duties of his position. He rose before dawn to supervise the P.T. sessions; he taught light-armor tactics in the classrooms; and he was always to be found beside the Assault Course when it was in use. He had inspected everything in the barracks by ten o'clock each day, was then received in audience by the Colonel Commandant, and later interviewed the lesser authorities below him, the middle-aged Pay Corps Captain who held the post of Adjutant, the Quartermaster, old Dr. Cross, the M.O., and—though more deferentially and in the latter's own office—Major Seligman, the Chief Tactical Instructor.

His clerks admired him and were frightened of his astonishing memory; the N.C.O. drill-and-weapon instructors approved of his meticulous attention to detail; and the cadets, of course, were terrified of him. He sometimes stood in for the Colonel Commandant, an exceptionally lazy man even by Regular Army standards, at the full-dress Saturday parades; and when he did so he invariably turned up on horseback, a big, glittering figure rigidly poised on his beautiful Arab mare, taking the salute from the companies of white-belted cadets marching past behind their officers.

Now, he ordered a brandy-and-soda from the Egyptian barman, slid onto a vacant stool beside the Hussar Major, and said again, "What if this was Sandhurst, Hood?"

"I was saying, sir, that if this was Sandhurst one of my cadets would have a very sore behind, and deservedly so."

Exelfield signed the slip of paper which the barman slid deferentially toward him and asked, "Which particular cadet?"

"You've probably seen him, sir, on parade. A boy called Van der Haar."

"Ah, yes, yes. Yusef, give me some more ice. Yes, Van der Haar. He's here for Intelligence. They want him in Syria, apparently. They couldn't actually commission him direct because he's only seventeen. He'll be eighteen by the time he leaves here, though." Despite the fact that there were at least six hundred cadets at the school, the Staff Major knew the details of an astonishing number of them, particularly of those who were of some special interest. "And you think that a sound beating would improve him? You're probably right; it improves so many things." He smiled. "Dogs, horses, boys—they're all the better for a taste of the whip."

"And women and walnut trees, or so the proverb says," added Seligman.

Lutwyche frowned. "No, but seriously, sir, Hood's quite right. Van der Haar's attitude's all wrong somehow; I don't quite know how to put it, but he's no idea how to behave like a soldier, and he doesn't seem to mind. It may not be entirely his fault, of course; he's a boy amongst a lot of grown men and they spoil him in consequence, so he thinks he can get away with anything—what with this stupid business of Intelligence pushing him through here without any service in the ranks and having a job all ready for him and so forth. But all the same, he's a bloody little nuisance. Hood's right; he wouldn't get away with it at Sandhurst, not for twenty-four hours."

Yesterday evening Van der Haar had argued with him over the solution of a sand-table exercise; not disrespectfully, of course, but with a lack of deference, a complete lack of that correct military subservience so apparent in the older cadets. Everything about Van der Haar, Captain Lutwyche often thought—and since Van der Haar was a good-looking boy and Lutwyche liked good-looking boys he thought about him a lot —seemed designed to proclaim that he was a civilian in uniform, not a proper soldier, and with no desire or intention of becoming one. Once commissioned and in Syria that was what he would be, of course, a uniformed civilian; but the training school existed to inculcate and to heighten the traditional British military attitudes, not to see them disregarded, flouted, almost, by seventeen-year-olds.

Exelfield swirled the brandy round his glass thoughtfully. At last he said slowly, "You could probably cane him if you really wanted to, Lutwyche."

Later, Seligman was to remember that moment, was to remember it for the rest of his life. The early afternoon sun lying in bars across the polished floor of the bar; Yusef, the bar steward, carefully slicing a lemon on a little silver dish; the other three officers, all so different and yet all with one thing, their position as professional Regular soldiers, in common, at ease beside the bar; George VI staring down, smirking at them all from his heavy frame. The whole scene was so calm, so ordinary, so certainly the same as in dozens of other Officers' messes at half-past twelve on this weekday morning in wartime Egypt. And yet, surely at that moment an odd little flicker of apprehension had passed through him; almost, it seemed later, a premonition, a foreboding of something dark approaching, though still far off.

He had laughed though, he remembered, and said, "What nonsense, Exelfield! And anyway that sort of thing's all out, even at Sandhurst, today."

But the Staff Major had shaken his head. "No, I'm right I think. I believe it could be done. You like to take a bet on it, Seligman? Twenty-five pounds?"

"Good God, no! I wouldn't put it past you to waylay the fellow—with Hood's help, probably—in a dark corner, set about him with that riding crop of yours, and then come and claim your money!"

Lutwyche and Hood laughed dutifully, but Exelfield shook his head again and then began one of those carefully theoretical—surely it had still been theoretical at that stage—explanations of obscure peacetime Army regulations of which he was so fond. Seligman had not paid much attention; peacetime Army regulations bored him—he had enough to do keeping abreast of all the new wartime ones—and besides, his leg was hurting him again. It had all been something to do with rules about the age of enlistment; the fact that young Van der Haar, joining at seventeen, must have been taken on as a "boy" rather than as a "man." In the end he cut his fellow Major short by ordering another round of drinks.

When they came, Lutwyche said, "Very pretty, sir, but it doesn't add up. Van der Haar may be an Army 'boy' in Kings Regulations, but he's also a cadet sent here for special reasons. Can't you imagine the explosion there'd be if we caned a cadet? The heavens would fall!"

Exelfield lifted his narrow face and the light from the high window above the bar caught his pale eyes in a sudden glitter, so that for a moment they appeared transparent, like glass, as if one could see right through them. "It's just because he *is* a cadet that you could do it. For that matter, it's only because Intelligence slipped him in here as a cadet that he's in the Army at all. I suppose the fact of his age was officially over-looked, but that doesn't alter King's Regulations. By military law Van der Haar is an Army 'boy' and can be treated as such, as I've just explained." He smiled. "I bet his Intelligence friends didn't know that one."

"But even so . . ."

"You think there'd be trouble? Why? I know that this is supposed to be a *people's war,* as they say. But if that expression means anything at all, which I doubt, it means equality and democracy and no privileges or favoritism—all that balls."

The two Guardsmen snorted; they had all the Regular officer's contempt for the huge mass of wartime soldiers, so many of whom, backed by Socialist politicians, seemed bent on sullying the pure well of peace-time military traditions.

Exelfield nodded and continued. "Well, how could that sort of thing be invoked to protect Van der Haar? Boys who are getting special treatment and privileged safe jobs are *not* the heroes of the people or the popular press."

Despite an instinctive antipathy toward the Staff Major, Seligman was intrigued by this argument, which had left the uninteresting and, to him, unknown subjects of what could or could not happen in peace-time at Sandhurst and had taken on a political slant. He said, "I see your point as far as the outside con-census of opinion is concerned; and, of course, you're quite right."

Exelfield nodded acknowledgment. "But, in fact, there's more in it than that. Cadets have no status while they are here. They are neither officers, N.C.O.'s, nor privates. Until they achieve their commissions or revert to their former ranks they have no official status at all, and Van der Haar least of all, I imagine. He's a complete anomaly."

"Intelligence probably don't think so."

"What they think or don't think doesn't matter. While he's here he belongs to us, to Lutwyche, rather."

"Poor Lutwyche!"

"And Lutwyche can do what he likes with him, in-cluding caning him. King's Regulations lay down that it's perfectly legal up to the age of eighteen, as I've just explained." Exelfield eased his shoulders under his tight tunic. "But, anyway, it wouldn't be necessary to go into all that. Van der Haar wouldn't know whether it was a legal punishment or not. And you know what the cadets are like, they're so slavishly frightened of us that they accept everything we do to them. If Lutwyche was to put Van der Haar on a charge and have him up in the office and tell him that he was going to be caned, and that because of his age and K.R. article XYZ of 1905 or something it was a perfectly legal and proper punishment, well, what do you suppose he'd say?"

Seligman stirred restively on his stool. "He'd demand to see the Commandant, obviously."

Exelfield shook his head. "I should think that extremely unlikely. He might, of course, but he probably doesn't even know that he's allowed to. And what if the Commandant agreed with Lutwyche—and from what I know of him he certainly would—what then?"

"I supposed Van der Haar would have to ask for a court martial."

But the idea was so ludicrous that everyone laughed.

Exelfield said, "Oh, I admit that if the matter went up to higher authority it wouldn't be permitted, even though it is legal. But Van der Haar wouldn't do that. Firstly, he doesn't know how to and no other cadet would dare to help him, and secondly, he'd never dare go over Lutwyche's head in the matter, because if he did, we'd throw him out. He's theoretically an infantryman, you know. Do you suppose—when it was explained to him—that he'd prefer to lose his job in Syria and be sent to a regiment he's never even seen as an ordinary fighting private, rather than . . ."

Hood said, "By God, I believe we're really onto something! I believe it could be done." The unconcealed pleasure and excitement in the young Lieutenant's voice shocked Major Seligman.

"Really, Hood," he began, but Lutwyche cut in.

"And anyway he *is* on a charge. He's coming up before me tomorrow. Sir, shall I try it? Or have you been pulling our legs?"

"I never pull anyone's leg," said the Staff Major coldly. He eyed his empty glass and motioned Yusef to refill it. "Only, for God's sake, check his age first. If he's a day over eighteen you can't do it; if he's a day under you can." He paused reflectively. "In any case it will be an amusing tactical exercise in psychology. If you talk to the Commandant first you can probably tell Van der Haar that he can take his choice of being caned or thrown out. His reactions should be interesting."

Seligman said angrily, "It isn't a choice at all! You know perfectly well he'll have to ..."

"Exactly!" Hood's voice was jubilant. "That's the whole point, isn't it?" In his excitement he had missed the implications in Seligman's tone.

Now, the Major said disgustedly, "What do you want to cane this wretched boy for, anyway? Are you all sadists or something?"

There was a momentary shocked silence and Seligman felt the attitudes of the other three officers hardening against him. Despite the fact of his field rank— he was more than a year senior to Exelfield—he was not a professional soldier, and they were.

At last, his quiet precise voice holding a coolly offended note, Lutwyche said, "It's not a question of wanting to, sir. That's not the point at all. It's just that a dose of the cane is exactly the right thing for Van der Haar at the moment. It's what he needs."

Seligman grinned humorlessly. "The cane as a cure-all, in fact. It's truly amazing what some people think it can do."

Dryly, Exelfield said, "And it's truly amazing what it *can* do, too." He glanced for a moment at the Hussar Major beside him, and once more the latter received the impression that those pale eyes were quite transparent, that he was looking through them right into the depths of Exelfield's head and seeing only blackness.

22

With a conviction which he did not entirely feel, Seligman said, "They won't let you get away with it in any case. It's out of the question altogether."

"You think so?"

"I know so. We live in the nineteen-forties, not the eighteen-forties. You forget that."

"But you aren't prepared to back your judgment?"

"Yes, of course, I am. All right, all right! Twenty-five pounds, fifty, if you like."

"I'll take you." The Staff Major slipped a small note-book from a pocket of his tunic and scribbled the figure. Looking up, he asked suddenly, "Tell me, were you never caned at school?"

"No, thank God!" Seligman shuddered. "The whole thing gives me the creeps." He rose with a sigh, wincing a little as his damaged leg took the pressure of his weight. "And now I'm going to wash for lunch."

NEXT DAY at noon three cadets were standing outside "E" Company office, while Company Sergeant-major Ross waited beside the door for Captain Lutwyche to be ready to deal with them. They were all up on charges for what, by outside Army standards, were offences so trivial that they would have been dealt with, if indeed noticed at all, by a brief rebuke from an N.C.O. But under the tensely rigid discipline of the training school, even an improperly rolled shirt sleeve or a crumpled collar meant a charge on the company report and was punished with at least one rigorous, exhausting extra hour of drill.

Two of the cadets were husky young men, ex-sergeants in their mid-twenties. Practically all the cadets at the school had been N.C.O.'s, and although they removed their rank badges on entering the training school and replaced them by white bars on their shoulders, most men's shirts still bore in dark outline the mark of noncommissioned stripes. Van der Haar, standing beside the two ex-sergeants, was conspicuous for several things—far too conspicuous, as Captain Lutwyche often thought—and one of them was the lack of such dark patches on his new sand-colored shirt. And, though it was not his fault, his shirts and trousers should have been of British khaki, not of American beige drill. Yet, since the British stocks had been exhausted and replaced by this cloth at the time he entered the school, there had been nothing else in which to dress him. Now he stood out on parade, a pale beige figure in the lines of faded greenish khaki. Captain Lutwyche disapproved of this, too.

Van der Haar had been within a little more than three months of his eighteenth birthday when he entered the training school, and the authorities who wanted him in Syria would have preferred it if his birthday had already been passed. But one of the four-monthly training courses was about to commence and the matter of his age, like many other things, was officially disregarded. Now, he had been a cadet for nearly three months and the first harsh shock of Army life, and life in an officer-training school at that, had partly worn off. But it had left its mark as Major Seligman and Captain Lutwyche both in their different ways noticed. The thin dark boy who had arrived so surprisingly in civilian clothes at the beginning of the course was still darker now, as heavily bronzed as the other desert soldiers by the fierce sun under which the cadets daily wheeled and stamped across the parade ground; and despite the prediction of Mr. Ulick, the Brigade Sergeant-major, that drilling and plenty of good plain Army food filled a youngster out wonderfully, he did not seem to have put on any weight. He was perpetually smiling, except on parade—Ulick had managed to correct that fault—but it was a smile which covered fear and apprehension, a mask to disguise the dismay of someone lost, hopelessly, irretrievably lost in a foreign land whose ways he did not know, whose language he did not speak, and of whose intricate and savagely enforced laws he had not the slightest understanding.

Everybody had made allowances, as far as they personally could, for the boy; but in an establishment such as this they had to be made clandestinely, for there was no way of relaxing the rigid military discipline for one man, whatever the circumstances. As individuals, most of the staff would have wished to be kind to Van der Haar, but in their professional capacities they could not be so. He had to be shouted at on the parade ground as much as any other cadet; he had to be officially chased on the square, officially bullied by the N.C.O. instructors, officially harried by the authorities. The system said that this was the way to train officers; it could not be altered. To the other cadets—ex-sergeant-majors, sergeants, and corporals, combat soldiers who had often been years in the army —this treatment meant nothing; they knew it for the bluff it was. Van der Haar never properly understood this; when he was shouted at he thought the shouter was really angry, really hating him. Major Seligman had told Mr. Ulick that it was extremely cruel to have sent the boy to the training school without any previous experience of the far-more-easy-going life of the Army outside; and Ulick, who despite his bulk, red face, and terrifying voice was a kindly man, had fully

25

agreed. For Van der Haar could never, it seemed, acquire that peculiar military patina, that odd, illusive gloss of bearing and speech which marked the British Regular soldier and upon which, even now in the middle of a war, the authorities at the training school set so high a premium.

As his first dazed fear lessened, as he found that he was still alive and that whatever the treatment to which he was being subjected betokened, it did not, apparently, indicate power-crazy hatred, he reverted naturally to the modes of thought and expression of an intelligent middle-class adolescent from a civilian and cosmopolitan background. He was invariably polite to everyone, but with the sort of hesitant civilian politeness which indicated that he was a person in his own right and ought to be treated as such, and not—as he actually was—a mere cipher, Number 8509654, Private Van der Haar, M.J.

Despite the fact that he had rapidly attained the speckless, glinting, polished turnout that was demanded of all cadets and, somewhat more tardily, acquired the necessary yogalike ability to stand motionless at rigid attention for long periods of time, he somehow remained—obscurely, illusively but very certainly—an outsider, a civilian in uniform.

And he *knew* nothing—nothing at all. His ignorance of every aspect of military life was abysmal. He had been told to ask questions, of course, but no one quite expected the sort of questions he asked: "I met a man in a corridor who was wearing three stars and a crown on his shoulders, what would he be?" "Why does the officer who limps wear red trousers?" "What does L.M.G. stand for?" "What is a casualty return?" "What are King's Regulations?" And the trouble was that however sincere such absurdly elementary questions might be—in fact, just because they were so absurdly elementary—they generally sent a gale of laughter through a classroom, laughter in which Van der Haar too often joined. It was like having an ignorant child about the place.

Too often, also, his questions, his mistakes, his apologies and smiling corrections seemed—unintentionally it was to be hoped, of course—to throw an unflattering light upon some illogical but sacred tradition of the Army. And soon Van der Haar's very presence, an awed and frightened heathen amongst the faithful, began to grate more and more upon the Regular officers who saw aspects of their chosen profession being brought, however innocently, into question, perhaps even ridicule, by the necessity of having to explain them in the simplest terms to a uniformed soldier without either rank or experience.

They, too of course, had made allowances up to a point—they could not very well have done otherwise —but unwillingly and in the hope that it would only be for the shortest possible time; for surely no one, not even a seventeen-year-old boy from some obscure home in the Levant who was sent up for an officer's commission, could know absolutely *nothing at all* about the British Army. But such, in fact, was the case.

"He literally doesn't know one end of a rifle from the other!" Captain Lutwyche had said in shocked amazement after the first few days. And his amazement and shock were genuine, for despite—or perhaps because of—his unsoldierly looks and unstable temperament, Lutwyche was a rigid martinet on professional matters and "E" company was the best and smartest in the training school.

"He's got to learn," Hood had said ominously, and had personally put Van der Haar through hours of extra rifle drill until the boy's hands were bruised and bloody, his face a dull gray with exhaustion. "It's almost as tiring for me," Hood had said in the mess, "but it's got to be done. He's got to learn."

But if rifle drill could be taught in that way, there were other things which could not: intangible things, attitudes of mind, outlook, beliefs—all the more important things, in fact, which went to make up the traditional British officer. To all of these Van der Haar appeared completely oblivious. And as the weeks had passed, the patience of the officer instructors had worn thin. They themselves, when at Sandhurst, had taken far less time to get down to military life; a week, two weeks, and surely they had understood things which Van der Haar, after practically three months, still failed to grasp. That they themselves had chosen military careers, that they mostly came from military families, had been to English public schools with Officer Training Corps and military traditions and were therefore mentally highly attuned to military life by the time they were eighteen—whereas Van der Haar had no such background—this they took no account of. If Van der Haar had not altered his civilian outlook after three months of intensive training, then he was not trying to change it, was deliberately retaining it, taking pleasure in mocking the Army as, the officers reminded themselves grimly, many civilians had done before the war; but now things were going to be different for the mockers who were in their power; the tables were turned.

They punished him with extra drill parades, which only had the effect of tiring him still more and adding to the nervous exhaustion that too often seemed to break out in laughter at the wrong time. They would have liked to have rejected him and turned him out of the training school as "unfit officer material," which by their standards he undoubtedly was; but though

Van der Haar did not know this—and they took care that he should not—such a step would not have been easy to take, and would have been hotly contested by the Intelligence department that wished to employ him. There had seemed, exasperatingly, no way of doing anything about Van der Haar until the unexpected turn the conversation in the officers' bar had taken yesterday before lunch.

Captain Lutwyche polished off the first two cadets in short order: two hours' extra drill and for God's sake to remember that they were here to become officers and that they themselves would soon command men and that how, for God's sake, did they think they could win the respect of those men if they did not show regard for proper discipline and good order themselves and, for God's sake, to remember this. In any case they had promptly pleaded guilty to the charges against them: dirty bayonet and dirty rifle, respectively; though by any standards save those of the training school both bayonet and rifle had been immaculate.

When Van der Haar was brought in, Lutwyche, his head bent over his desk, was studiously writing. He did not look up, but merely said, "All right, Sar'nt-major. I want to speak to this cadet alone. You can wait outside."

"Sir!" snapped Ross by way of acknowledgement; he saluted, turned about, and stamped out of the room.

For several more moments Lutwyche did not look up. He was worried, obscurely agitated, and acutely conscious both of the presence of the boy standing silently in front of his table and of his own mixed feelings, in which a sense of excited guilt played a strong part. The whole thing, Lutwyche admitted to himself, seemed somehow to have gotten out of hand in the

29

last twenty-four hours. For despite the remarks of Exelfield before lunch yesterday, the matter was not to be as simple as anyone had then thought. Lutwyche's own idea, based on his school and Sandhurst days, had been to treat Van der Haar in the same way as other boys, who did not readily conform to traditional behavior patterns, had been treated in those places. He had expected that this morning he would be able to send for Hood at the same time as he dismissed Ross. Then, in the presence of the Lieutenant alone, he would have given Van der Haar an angry, firm, and righteous lecture on his shortcomings and lack of military spirit—or, rather, lack of respect for it, for the spirit itself was not an easy thing to define to a civilian. He would have briefly informed the cadet what was going to be done about it, stressing the point that since Van der Haar was a boy—and behaved like one —rather than a man, he would be punished like a boy rather than a man. Then this table would have been pushed into the middle of the room, Van der Haar told to bend over it, and Hood, who was only five years older and in some ways the equivalent of the boy's cadet-captain had they been at Sandhurst, would have administered a dozen sharp strokes with one of the leather-covered canes all the officers carried on parade. After a further short lecture to drive the reason for the punishment home, Van der Haar could have been dismissed. And Lutwyche, who believed in the soundness of such methods, would have confidently awaited the boy's subsequent improvement.

But when, on Exelfield's advice, he had approached the Commandant—a tall handsome Guards colonel, a man of great personal charm whose mild, soft-voiced manner and tolerantly amused outlook hid a steely determination to uphold every outmoded aristocratic tradition of the British officer caste—Lutwyche had found that things were not to be like that at all. Not that the Colonel Commandant was against the idea in itself.

"It's really rather a pity that the Army ever dropped flogging as a punishment, don't you think?" he asked, smiling his singularly sweet smile; and Lutwyche, as on several previous occasions, had not been quite certain that the Colonel was joking. "But the fact is, my good Captain Lutwyche, that this place is *not* Sandhurst. You have only to look at the cadets, far less to listen to them speak, to realize that. We are trying to turn N.C.O. material into officer material which, as I once pointed out, is like trying to turn chalk into cheese. Very good chalk and very useful as *chalk,* but it makes a most indifferent substitute for cheese, I'm afraid. We do our best, of course, as we must; but it really cannot be pretended that we are teaching an establishment of quite carefully selected young gentlemen the profession of an Army officer."

"With respect, Colonel," Lutwyche had offered, "I don't think young Van der Haar could be considered N.C.O. material."

"I'm sure he couldn't, my dear fellow. And, of course, he's not really officer material either. But then, as I understand it, he's here for special reasons, an Intelligence job or something." The Colonel's mouth turned down slightly at the corners in distaste. "However, that, I'm happy to say, is not our affair. The fact remains that you think he should be caned and Exelfield apparently thinks so, too, and says that in the circumstances it is perfectly legal and proper, so naturally I concur. From what you have told me, I have no doubt that it will be just that—that significant experience, one might say, of which this youth appears to stand in need. However, you can't do it yourself, nor can

Hood. Van der Haar, unlike a Sandhurst cadet, is an enlisted man, or boy, rather, as Exelfield accurately says. Consequently, it's an N.C.O.'s job to do the actual caning, your C.S.M. Ross, I imagine. Anyway, the man to see about it is Ulick; he'll know the drill. And now, I must admit to being rather busy. . . ."

Ulick had stared at him almost unbelievingly for a moment, and Lutwyche had somehow felt it necessary —though in fact he knew that he should not have done so—to explain everything to the Brigade Sergeant-major, to justify the matter in detail and with as much righteous anger as he could summon up. And at the end, all Ulick had done, of course, was to snap, "Yessir!"

"Well, the fact is, Mr. Ulick," Lutwyche had said, unhappily aware of the other's deep disapproval, "that you—er—you know the drill I understand?"

"Yessir."

"You've—seen it done?"

"Yessir. Four times in all, if I remember rightly."

"Could you tell me, briefly, please, the way it is? Where, for instance, does it take place?"

In the gymnasium, sir. The boy is held over the vaulting horse by two sergeants and his company sergeant-major administers the ordered number of strokes in the presence of the boy's platoon officer, company commander, myself, and an officer representing the Colonel—the Adjutant usually, sir, or in this case probably the Staff Major. Afterward the boy is taken to the Medical Inspection room to be examined and treated, if necessary."

"Good God!" Lutwyche had exclaimed faintly, and had seen, or thought he had seen, a sardonic gleam of satisfaction in Ulick's officially motionless gray eyes. "Well, that wasn't how I thought of it at all. . . ." He had rattled a ruler against the edge of his desk and suddenly, surprisingly, Ulick had barked, "Sir, permission to speak, sir?"

"Of course, Mr. Ulick," Lutwyche had said a trifle too eagerly. "Please say anything you want to."

"With respect, sir, I don't think this is the way to deal with Cadet Van der Haar. It's a punishment generally used only on enlisted Army boys—peacetime Regulars, sir, and you knows what they can be like—who've been found guilty of continuous insubordinate and unruly behavior. I don't think this cadet comes into that category. I think . . ."

"No, no, of course not, no. But carry on, Mr. Ulick, please. What were you going to say?"

"I think he tries his best to do well, sir. It's just that he's—he's not cut out for the military life, sir. And that's not his fault, sir."

"Yes, yes, yes," Lutwyche had said tiredly. "We've been into that carefully, I and the Staff Major and Lieutenant Hood." He had pulled himself upright in his chair, remembering that he was an officer and must show firmness of decision. And anyway, the Colonel apparently wanted it done; he could not back out now even if he wanted to, and somewhere deep in his being something told him that he did not want to, that this would at least add a spice of excitement to the dullness of the daily routine. "The fact remains that this type of punishment has been decided upon after much careful thought, and must therefore be carried out." The impersonal phrasing of this had encouraged him considerably. "I'm sorry it can't be done more informally, as at Sandhurst, but there it is; regulations must be obeyed. As far as Van der Haar goes"—he had hesitated, looking down at his desk, and then remembered the Colonel's words—"well, it will be a significant experience and I don't suppose we'll have any more trouble from him for the remainder of his time here. All right, Mr. Ulick. Six o'clock this evening in the gym, then. I'll tell the other officers and you will see to all the other necessary arrangements. Oh, and I think you'd better see Van der Haar after Company Office and—er—explain the drill to him."

"Yessir."

And now, here was Van der Haar, a small still figure, very neat this morning, standing in front of him, and the Staff Major's psychologically interesting experiment must be commenced. Lutwyche put down his pencil at last and looked up, frowning. For a second his eyes met Van der Haar's big, dark, troubled ones, and moved over the smooth oval of the boy's face—even though he was nearly eighteen he still had no reason to shave—noting a blue bruise on one cheekbone, a result of being flung over the wall of the Assault Course, and the childishly full-lipped mouth. Physically, Van der Haar held a strong attraction for Lutwyche, a fact which alternately exhilarated and frightened the Captain, who was usually careful to conduct his peculiar and infrequent love affairs with young men of his own social class—which Van der Haar was not. Unfortunately, the boy possessed the slender, dark good looks which so often come to the male youth of the warmer southern nations during adolescence, a quickly passing, illusive, sexless radiance seldom encountered amongst the fair-skinned nations of the north. Since in all other respects Lutwyche was a conventional man, he was often miserably unhappy about the carefully hidden sexual inversion of which Van der Haar's proximity so powerfully reminded him; and since he had been reared in all the peculiar arrogant puritanism of the British ruling classes, he often felt, obscurely, that in punishing Van der Haar, he was in some way atoning for the defect in his own nature. Besides, Van der Haar, dripping with sweat on the parade ground or covered in dust and dirt at the end of the Assault Course, was a distinctly less attractive figure than the boy in the bright clean shirt and shorts and glittering white belt who stood before him this morning.

And now—he lowered his eyes, then lifted them once more to Van der Haar's face. It was certainly not the face of a boy prone to continuous insubordinate and unruly behavior, nor was it remotely the face of a Sandhurst cadet; it was still in many ways the face of a child. Lutwyche suddenly knew that Ulick's estimation of Van der Haar had been completely right, while his own and that of Hood were completely wrong. But that could not make any difference now. He took a deep breath and began with an effort on the speech he had decided to make earlier in the day.

"Van der Haar, you're up on a charge of idleness and unsoldierly conduct in that Lieutenant Hood found your locker in a disgracefully disordered condition on his inspection yesterday morning. But I'm not going to go into that now. I've got something else to say to you, which is why I asked Sergeant-major Ross to leave us alone. The fact is that your whole behavior since you've been here, your whole attitude and outlook have been not merely unsatisfactory but *increasingly* so. Now we all know that you are *new* to Army life and that you're a lot younger than the other cadets and that you have not had their experience. And because of that we've all—all of us on the staff here—made continual allowances for you. We have been exceedingly patient, far too patient, I'm afraid. But instead of co-operating with us or making any sort of real *effort* to adapt yourself . . ." It was surprising how easy it was when once he'd got started, Lutwyche thought. He found himself listening to his own voice with little more effort than if it had been a phonograph record. ". . . and since apparently nothing will prevent you from behaving in the way you do and failing even to try to improve, we have no option but to deal with you severely. We could easily return you to the unit to which you are accredited"—he paused a moment—"You do realize that, don't you?"

Van der Haar said, "Yes, sir."

"We could do that, but we don't want to and I don't suppose you want us to. Do you?"

"No, sir."

"I don't think you'd like being an ordinary private in a line of regiment for the rest of the war—or until you were killed—whichever is the shorter as the lawyers say." Lutwyche smiled, grimly he hoped, and saw fear flicker in the boy's dark eyes. "You wouldn't want that, would you?"

Van der Haar swallowed and said with difficulty, "No, sir."

"No, I imagine not." Lutwyche paused to let the effect sink in, and on the other side of the table Van der Haar shifted his feet, remembered that he was at attention, and stiffened again. He was frightened and unhappy, but as he had been in that condition for nearly three months he was coming to accept it as an apparently permanent state.

Van der Haar was the only child of a shabby Dutch-English middle-class family, who for two generations had lived and intermarried with the Syrian French. They owned a small import-export business in Beirut, and before the First War they had been fairly prosperous; but the business had run down badly during the twenties and thirties; there had not been enough money to send the boy to school in England, and instead he had received his education among the sons of minor French officials and businessmen in the free, French-run schools of the city. Thus, despite his consulate-registered birth certificate and passport, he was by environment and upbringing largely French—and Levantine French at that.

The family had left Syria after the defeat of France in 1940, and had come to Egypt with little money and poor prospects. The father had managed to find a job in Alexandria and there they had lived until Syria had fallen to the British and it had been possible to return. The Van der Haar business was almost ruined, and while the father patiently tried to pick up the pieces, his son had to be found an occupation. This was by no means easy; the British were now violently unpopular in conquered Syria amongst their ex-allies, and no one wanted to employ the boy until a lieutenant-colonel of Intelligence, who had become acquainted with the family in Alexandria and who needed a French-speaking officer on his staff, had suggested the Army. Van der Haar was completely bilingual; he often seemed to think in French, for when he was excited his English speech became oddly foreign; and he spoke a considerable quantity of Syrian Arabic as well. He was just what Colonel Dollond wanted as a junior assistant in fact, but when it came to the point, Army headquarters either could not or would not commission someone of seventeen without any previous training whatever, not even for the Intelligence Corps. Someone in authority, anxious to help, had suggested sending the boy to an officer-training school for four months; by the time he emerged, he would be eighteen and have at least a certain claim to be considered a soldier. Colonel Dollond had agreed and so had Van der Haar's father, and the boy in his best suit—the only one he possessed which had long trousers—had been sent back to Egypt and had fallen at once into a world of nightmare unreality, unlike anything he had ever conceived of knowing.

After the first week he had fully intended to run away, to escape somehow into the sane world beyond the barrack gates. It was then that he received a letter from Dollond saying that the Colonel was in the city and would like to see him on his next free afternoon. Since Colonel Dolland had gotten him into this terrifying place, Van der Haar assumed he could also get him out of it. He had rushed round to Dollond's hotel at the earliest moment and there, in the Colonel's big comfortable room—so reassuring after the prison bleakness of the barracks—had poured out his fear and misery and demanded release. Dollond, a small neat man hardly taller or broader than the young cadet who stood before him, had been sympathetic and worried.

"But Michael, you *had* to come here. I told you they wouldn't give you this job with me otherwise; I told you that, didn't I?"

"Yes, but I didn't know! I didn't know what it was going to be like! I—look, I don't mind about the job, Colonel Dollond. I'm sorry; I don't want it. I want to go home; please let me go home! I don't want to join the English Army."

"But, you *have* joined the Army."

"No, not till I'm made an officer and come to you. At present they say I'm not anything. They say they can throw me out if they want to, so I can't be in the Army, can I? Not properly in, I mean."

Dollond had risen and, taking Van der Haar's hand, had led him to a sofa and pulled him down beside him. "Now listen, Michael, while I explain. You *are* in the Army now. You're in it and I'm afraid you can't get out, not till the end of the war. And no one knows when that will be." And carefully, sympathetically, he had explained the situation, had urged the boy to go back and be patient. "It's only for four months. Rather less now, after all."

But four months to a seventeen-year-old is almost four years, and to Van der Haar each day at the training school seemed a year in itself. Yet he saw with dreadful, bleak clarity that there was no way out. The gates had clashed shut behind him, trapping him completely, horribly. Those gates would open only to send him back home to Syria and Dollond, or else as an ordinary private to some English regiment and probable death or mutilation in battle. The latter, at least, he had determined to avoid. On range-firing practice he had stolen a live cartridge from the canister at the pits, and this he kept carefully concealed, changing its hiding place at intervals, but never far from him. He did not doubt that he would use it if necessary, for despite the amused kindliness of the other cadets, he was not of their world nor they of his, and they could not help him. He was a stranger and afraid. He could have killed himself easily on almost any day of the last three months—or so he believed.

Besides, the cadets were one thing; the staff was quite another. He was so frightened of the staff that he no longer considered them as human beings but as some sort of devils, a race apart. He feared the Staff Major in particular—who, like Satan, seemed always just behind his shoulder, watching him—in the way superstitious peasants fear evil spirits on a lonely road at night, with an uncomprehending panic dread. But he felt much the same way about all the rest, except for Hood and Lutwyche—both of whom he hated so much that at times he almost forgot to fear them. At his school in Beirut the older boys had invariably shown kindness and help toward their juniors, and Van der Haar had grown up in the un-British belief that this was as it should be; youth should call to youth and because Hood, at twenty-three, was the youngest of his overseers Van der Haar had automatically expected kindness from him. Instead of which Hood, older, stronger, and infinitely better placed than himself, was more brutal toward him than any of the other staff. And sometimes it seemed, obscurely, to Van der Haar that Hood felt that he had to behave in this way, that it was expected of him, and that Hood's experience, unlike his own, had been in places where the older boys felt it their duty to systematically abuse and humiliate the younger and weaker ones—for their own good. "For your own good"; it was a phrase Hood often used, he had noted.

Yet Lutwyche was worse. Lutwyche appeared to be playing an odd, spidery sort of game with him; a mixture of high-minded lectures, continual soft-voiced corrections, and more-or-less-overt torture. The Captain seemed unable to let him alone; at every morning inspection those long cool fingers moved over him, smoothing his collar, adjusting his belt, squaring his white shoulder tabs. Even at chance meetings in the long corridors of the barracks Lutwyche would call him up for the same purpose. "Come here, Van der Haar. . . ."

Lutwyche had once made him stand out in the open sun with his rifle at full stretch above his head for nearly half an hour, and had shouted furiously at any movement of his trembling, dripping body. At last, when on the point of collapse, he had been pulled into a nearby storeroom Lutwyche had told him to sit down and had himself brought him a glass of water. He had stood over him, smiling his odd, small smile, and had said, "I didn't like doing that to you, Van der Haar, but it was necessary. A painful necessity to teach you to stand still on parade." But Van der

Haar knew that he had been lying; he had liked doing it.

Then there had been the time of the night exercise out in the desert. Van der Haar had been posted alone behind a light machine gun sited in a small declivity between two rocks, the big Egyptian moon bathing the desert in calm silver. Lutwyche had come silently up over the soft sand and had sat down beside him.

"Everything all right?"

"Yes, sir."

There had been a long pause, but Lutwyche had not gone away. At last he had said in his soft, precise voice, "You find all this—this life here—very unpleasant, don't you Michael?"

And Van der Haar, motionless, still staring fixedly over his gun, had felt a cool hand laid on his bare knee. He had swallowed, saying nothing and Lutwyche had waited a moment and then asked, plaintively, almost, it had seemed, "You don't like any of us very much, do you?" And the hand had moved further up his thigh, pushing gently under his shorts. Van der Haar had shivered convulsively—it was like the touch of a snake—and Lutwyche had removed his hand and gone away on his rubber-soled suède boots as quietly as he had come. Lutwyche was the worst of all.

Now, he looked across the table at Lutwyche and waited uneasily and in growing fear. The Captain was smiling and that was, as he now knew, a bad sign. At last, shifting some papers to one side and lowering his eyes for a second, Lutwyche said, still more quietly than usual, "We've decided this time to drive the lesson home firmly." He paused and Van der Haar, mystified, asked, "What lesson, sir?"

"Oh, *God!* God give me patience!" It was almost an explosion. "Haven't you listened to *anything* I've just said?"

"Yes, but . . ."

"I tell you! You're behaving improperly, in an unsoldierly way, all the time! You don't try! You continually behave like a civilian; you don't *try* to be a soldier! Well, we're going to *make* you! You're going to be caned. You'll get twelve strokes, and—and you'd better bloody well watch your step in future!" Lutwyche glared across the table red-faced, breathless, angry, but glad to have got it out.

Van der Haar shook his head dazedly. He had little idea what Lutwyche had been talking about; the remarks about caning hadn't sunk in properly.

Lutwyche saw this and was relieved. B.S.M. Ulick could do the explaining. He said quickly, "You're to report at once to the B.S.M.'s office; he's waiting for you. Very well. Dismiss!"

*T*HREE MINUTES later Van der Haar entered the Brigade Sergeant-major's office and saluted. "Captain Lutwyche told me to report to you, sir."

"Yes, I know." Ulick turned to his two clerks, "Corporal Barr! Corporal French! You can both fall out for ten minutes."

The two N.C.O.'s rose from their desks, brought their heels clicking to formal attention, and left the room. The Brigade Sergeant-major stared at the boy in the doorway, wondering what Lutwyche had said to him and guessing with the acuteness of the long-term N.C.O. that little had been explained. Van der Haar looked puzzled and nervous, but certainly not to the degree he would appear if—when—he knew what was in store for him. Lutwyche had passed the buck, and the B.S.M., silently cursing his superior officer, rose and walked round the desk, a bulky, heavy figure in his greenish khaki and brilliantly polished belt, who towered up, dwarfing the cadet still standing in the doorway.

"Yes, well, come in. Don't stand there. All right, you can stand easy." Correctly, Ulick should have called the boy Cadet Van der Haar, but in view of his youth—perhaps in view of what was going to be done to him—the B.S.M. found himself, heaven alone knew why, avoiding speaking his name. Instead, he asked, "What did . . . Did Captain Lutwyche tell you the punishment it's been decided to award you?"

Van der Haar nodded wordlessly. Then he swallowed and in an odd, shaky voice said, "I think they're going to flog me—or something."

Ulick made grunting noises of disapproval. "Cane you, not flog you."

"Are they different?"

"Flogging's been out for about the last eighty years, that's all." He suddenly realized that in all probability Van der Haar was thinking of some movie he had once seen: triangles on the barrack square, rows of stiff, red-coated soldiers, the falling lash and the rumble of drums to drown the screams of the victim. He said with an awkward effort at matter-of-factness, "This here's different, quite different, see? Nothing like flogging. Nobody's going to do that to you."

"Then what?"

Ulick sat upon the corner of his desk and tried to make the atmosphere a little less oppressive, a little more normal, by filling and lighting his pipe. It also gave him time to think. Over the flaming match

43

he asked, "You—surely when you was a nipper you had your sit-upon smacked, didn't you?"

The common English argot was not easily comprehensible to Van der Haar, but he grasped its gist. "No, no—never."

"But," the Sergeant-major persisted, "when you was a kid didn't you get into trouble, times? Break a window, cheek a copper, or something? No"—Ulick sighed—"I don't suppose you did. But you mean to tell me that even at school you was never caned? Never bent over and given a hiding?"

Van der Haar's sallow face flushed. "No, of course not." Then he felt he might have been impertinent, one had to be so careful of one's tone of voice here; everything had to be spoken dead level. "I am sorry, sir. No, nothing like that was ever done at my school. And not at home, naturally."

Ulick said grimly, "It's going to be done now, though."

"Why?"

It was a question which Ulick realized at once should certainly never have been asked and which it would be most improper for him to answer. Presumably, also, Captain Lutwyche had told Van der Haar why he was to be punished. Ulick opened his mouth to say, "That's none of my business," and then closed it again with the words unsaid. He felt, darkly but certainly, that the boy's question must be answered, and that in some mysterious, ill-defined way, nothing, none of the things in which he believed or in which he thought he believed—the Army, discipline, tradition, the barrack square—none of these would make sense any more if that answer could not be found and given.

A common man with little formal education, Ulick was nonetheless an acute observer of human beings and possessed an almost unparalleled experience of every side of Army life. Yet, as he sucked his pipe, his brow creased in thought, he became aware that if there was an answer to this question—and he saw increasingly clearly and uneasily what it was—it would be a dangerous one to put into the hands of the boy before him. Sensibly, however, Mr. Ulick had never regarded Van der Haar as an Englishman, but as a sort of foreigner with a remarkable fluency in the language; and it had been his experience that you could say things to foreigners which you would certainly think twice about saying to a fellow countryman. Englishmen had certain prejudices and beliefs never to be explained in words, most of which Ulick understood very well; foreigners did not appear to have any of these, at least in Ulick's experience, and they were prepared to discuss anything. They made good confidants.

Now, he blew out a cloud of smoke and said, "I don't know how it is where you comes from, of course —seems different, an' no harm in that. But if you'd been to one of the schools most English officers—Regulars, I means, of course—has been to, well, you'd know all about caning. And if you'd been to Sandhurst afterward, you'd have known all about it there, too. But you haven't been to those places, so you don't. All right." He paused, frowning, trying with all his might to do something he had never done before: to evaluate and analyze a social concept and to put the result into words. He knew the facts. He knew that the English upper-class, whom he thought of always in terms of "officers," put a peculiar and irrational value upon corporal punishment; it was almost an obsession with them, and practically every officer he had ever known "believed in it." Ulick believed in it himself, for that matter, but only as a means of correction and in cases where it was likely to work correctively; and in this, his attitude was both rational and typical of his working-class background. But he was also well aware that when the upper-class, the Regular officers whom it was his career to serve and therefore to study, made this statement of belief, they were not meaning what he meant. They believed in corporal punishment as a genuinely good thing in itself, a mystic ritual of pain and humiliation that possessed a special magical quality which could not fail to benefit, in some occult, inexplicable way, anyone below the statutory adult age. That there might be darker, far more complex factors behind this attitude Ulick only very dimly guessed—and quickly shied away from further exploration. At any rate, until today it had never struck him as odd that men to whom he invariably looked up, as being his better-educated and more intelligent superiors, should wholeheartedly support practices of exactly the same sort, and for exactly the same psychological reasons, as the barbaric initiation ceremonies of savage jungle tribes. He saw only that to them it was a class rite, and as such must be jealously retained, guarded, and worshiped. He knew all this, but he found that he could no more explain it to Van der Haar—foreigner or not —than he could explain another thing that he knew equally well: that the officers—and he guessed that it was not only Lutwyche behind this—wanted to cane Van der Harr not merely for being different from themselves but because he was very young and nervous and good-looking in his dark, smooth-skinned foreign way; and that because of all these things reacting upon their peculiar atavistic instincts they would greatly enjoy watching it done.

Now, taking his pipe from his mouth and staring at it as if he had never seen it before, he said, "What it amounts to is, well, it's been done to all of them, see? All the officers here. Done in different ways I expect, but done, all right. When they was boys. And they think it won't do you no harm to know what it's like, either."

Van der Haar said, "They don't do it to the others."

"The others is men. You're a boy."

Ulick abruptly slid off his desk and stood up. He knew that his explanation had not been a satisfactory one, but it was all he could give in the circumstances. And, as he reminded himself now, it was not his duty to explain that side of the matter. It was his duty to make sure that Van der Haar knew what to do in the gym this evening. He picked up a sheet of paper on which he had made notes earlier that morning and when he spoke, his voice was firm to the point of sternness.

"Now see here, young fellow, this business has been ordered and it's got to be done. Let's get that clear for a start, eh? You've only been in the Army three months, but that's quite long enough to learn that orders has to be carried out." He saw the boy nod and his shoulders lift in a shrug of resigned acceptance. "Right. Now this business isn't going to be any fun for anyone—not for us that has actually the doing of it, anyway. But if you'll just try to co-operate, see, we'll make it as easy an' quick for you as we can." And now he found it easier to look at his notes rather than at Van der Haar. "I've changed the drill a bit to make it simpler for you; the less you has to do the better. So there'll be no marching in and marching out. You report to me in the gym at ten to six in P.T. order. Sergeant-major Ross and two other sergeants will be there. We'll be all ready when the officers come at six. Now listen; you'll be standing between the two sergeants near the horse, see? I calls everyone to atten-

47

tion and report you present. Captain Lutwyche then
reads the sentence. How many was it?"

"How many?"

"Strokes of the cane."

"Twelve."

Van der Haar's voice sounded sick and Ulick did not
look up. "He reads out the sentence. I repeat it. Then
I says, 'Carry on, sir?' He says, 'Carry on, Sergeant-
major,' and—hmm—I'll have to change this next bit,
too, 'cos if you was an ordinary peacetime enlisted
'boy' I'd say 'Strip, an' get over the horse.' But as it is,
I think I'd just better give you a nod, see? All right.
You drops your trousers—you won't be wearing anything underneath them, of course—an' with a sergeant
on each side of you, you goes to the horse and bends
over it with your arms along the top. We'll have to
lower the horse to your height first, of course—must remember that. Then the two sergeants get a hold on
your arms; it's their job to hold you still, so don't
struggle against them 'cos you'll only hurt yourself. I
says to C.S.M. Ross, 'Twelve strokes, Sergeant-major,
carry on.' He says, 'Yessir.' I counts each one out loud,
and when we gets to twelve I'll say to you—quietlike,
of course—'All right, get up.' Then you goes back to
where you was and puts your trousers on. Then you
stands at ease—try to remember that, if you can. Then
I calls everyone to attention, salutes, and requests permission of the senior officer present to dismiss in the
ordinary way. He'll give it an' then—this is where I've
done a bit more changing—we stays where we *is;* we
don't none of us *move.* The officers will have to break
off and leave the gym when they see that we're standing still, and then—well, it's finished and done with,
and a good thing, too."

He looked up at last and his apprehensions of what
he would see were fully realized. Van der Haar was

staring at him in incredulous disbelief, his face a dark, fiery crimson. Ulick felt his heart sink; this business was going to be far worse than even he had imagined.

At last the cadet stuttered, "They—they're going to do *that* to *me!*" And then, suddenly, he came to life. Taking quick steps about the room, his narrow brown hands—hands which still bore the scars of Hood's extra rifle drill—opening and shutting, he started to talk furiously, hysterically; his accent and even his phrasing losing their usual careful English and becoming, to Ulick, unmistakably those of a foreigner speaking the language.

"No, no; it is impossible this! You do not understand. You do not understand at all! I am sent here because I am not quite old enough to work immediately for Colonel Dollond. It is not a question of the British Army—in that I am not interested or involved. My parents, my father—we are poor, you see, not rich like these English officers here, and I must have work. I have left school; I need work. So Colonel Dollond, whom we have met in Alexandria and who has been kind to us, suggests that I work for him as an assistant in his office. I speak French and Arabic, you see, and he needs this. So I am sent here for a little to learn about the Army, they say, but really to fill in time until I am eighteen. I am very sorry that I came. It was very wrong of them to send me. I see that now. It is all a very great mistake. If I have been a nuisance here then I am very sorry for that, too; I did not want to be a nuisance to anyone. I have tried to be good, all the time—but it is impossible! The whole thing is impossible. And now—and now!" He shook his head and his hands flew open in a gesture of despairing bewilderment.

Then, urgently, he swung round to the B.S.M. "I must find Colonel Dollond! I do not know where he is, but I must find him! He will explain to them on the telephone. He will explain about me and that it is all a mistake. I am sure none of them *know!* But *you* know, now. You will help me to find Colonel Dollond and everything will be explained, everything will be all right." As if self-hypnotized by his own words, his voice quietened and resumed its normal English tone. "Perhaps—yes, perhaps they will let me go home."

This exhibition was, of course, entirely unique in Mr. Ulick's long experience. Yet, as a senior Warrant Officer, he was accustomed to dealing with the unexpected. It was a part of his duties to be prepared to do so. He took Van der Haar firmly by the shoulder and sat him down in Corporal French's chair. "Stay there a moment." Then he went to a cupboard and, taking out a flask, filled a small glass with brandy and carried it carefully back to the boy. "Now drink this—all at once. That's better."

Van der Haar shuddered and coughed as the brandy burned his throat; then Ulick took the glass and put it carefully away. He paced the room twice and then turned to the cadet, noting that a more normal color had returned to the smooth olive face, the trembling had nearly died away.

"What you just said—if I was to repeat it, which I won't—would stop the—stop what you want stopped, all right. I can tell you that, lad! If any of the officers was to have heard you, you'd likely be out an' on your way back to your regiment in an hour's time." He paused. "Still, in a way I'm glad you said it because we—you an' I at least—knows where we stands; and there's never no harm in that. Now I'm going to tell *you* some things which you probably won't like; but they happens to be true, and if you just listen carefully—you

50

don't have to say anything, just listen—you'll understand. 'Cos you *can* understand. You're educated and you aren't a fool. I knows that well enough.

"Now first, I wants you to know that I *do* see how it all looks to you. I see exactly what's happened an' I think it's a bloody shame. I'm sorry for you, I tell you straight. I've never been sorrier for anyone in my life, 'far as I can remember." He took a deep breath, realizing that he had gone far enough in this direction; too much sympathy could very easily undo what good it lay within his power to attempt. "But you *are* in the Army, and you knows it well enough. This talk of letting you go home—that's just plain silly. You knows all right that can't happen. No, we got to get you through another four weeks in this place. Only four weeks, mind; and then, then off you goes to Syria and your Colonel Dolland and this job you want. It's all there waiting for you, isn't it? Just waiting at the end of four more weeks—thirty days or so. You've had a bad time, a real bad time, I know; but you can stand it for just that bit longer, can't you now?" His voice had become cajoling, persuasive. "Thirty more days, that's all. "It's not too bad now, is it? An' that job you want—that job in Syria where you'll be near home and your mum an' your dad. It won't be long now."

He saw Van der Haar nod and thought the boy's mouth seemed to lift a little in a weak smile. "Yes, that's it. But, look—we got to get this other business over first, see?" Ulick took a deep breath. "Now listen, the officers *wants* to do this to you. You don't know why an' I knows it doesn't make any sort of sense to you; I can see that well enough. But that's how it is. It's something they probably been wanting to do for a long time. They've fixed it so that if you try to stop them doing it, they'll throw you out. An' then—

good-bye to that job of yours and being near home and everything." He turned and put a hand on Van der Haar's shoulder. "Look, it's legal, see, because of your age. If you tried to go over their heads, well, it would be you against the rest of the Army from the Commander in Chief down; they'd fix you proper. So you've got to let them do it; an' if you can, you got to try not to make too much fuss. 'Cos if you can do that I think they'll likely let you alone for the rest of your time here. Once they've"—he spoke with an unaccustomed bitterness—"once they've had their bit of fun they'll feel guiltylike, I shouldn't wonder, 'cos they must know that . . . Anyway, they'll let you alone a bit to make up, see? An' then those thirty days won't be so bad at all. You just keep quiet and they'll go soon enough."

Van der Haar nodded and got slowly to his feet. He was looking calmer now and the trapped wild-animal glint had gone from his eyes. The brandy and Ulick's evocation of home had had their effect. And he had suddenly remembered his concealed bullet and realized that despite Ulick's words there was another choice open to him. Deep within him, he knew that it was not a true choice, but he intended, at least until six o'clock this evening, to pretend that it was. Now he said with a dull nonchalance, "I understand what you've told me about—about how it's going to be done. That was what you had to tell me? Why I was sent to you?"

"That's it." Uneasily, Ulick noted the tone of empty despair; uneasily, he remembered that there were more than five hours to go—the whole slow tropic afternoon, during much of which time the cadets were free to do what they liked inside the barracks —before the assignment at six o'clock. He did not know about the rifle bullet, but he accurately guessed the state of Van der Haar's mind, and there were plenty of other ways of doing it. He told himself that no sane person, even at seventeen, would commit suicide merely to avoid a couple of minutes of ferocious pain; but then he realized that Van der Haar had not even mentioned that side of the affair, and that it was quite possible that it bulked less largely in his thoughts than the fact of being forced to undress formally in front of the officers. For considering what he now knew—and what he suspected Lutwyche and Hood also knew—of this boy's background and character, he saw that what was to take place this evening was not merely a brutal piece of inhumanity, still less corrective punishment; it was a moral, and as close as possible to being a physical, rape.

And suddenly he felt tired—tireder than his normal, heavy day's routine ever left him, tireder than he had felt for years. He was tired of this stupid cruelty on the part of stupid officers, tired of the officers themselves, and more than anything else tired of Van der Haar, who unintentionally had made him question values, standards, and attitudes he had not questioned throughout his life and did not want to question now. Van der Haar was the direct cause of all this trouble and might yet be the cause of a lot more. He shook his head, strode back behind his desk, and sat down. "All right then, you can go now. Think about what I've said. And send Corporals Barr and French back here."

But, surprisingly, when a few seconds later the two Corporals entered the room, snapping to attention and saluting in the doorway, they found that Mr. Ulick was grinning to himself and shaking his head in wonderment. For he had just recalled that the unthinkable had happened: A seventeen-year-old soldier, with neither rank nor service, had informed a Brigade Sergeant-major of Cavalry to his face that, personally, he was neither interested nor involved in the British Army.

*W*HEN Sergeant Cole entered the gym that evening he found Sergeant Calderon of "C" Company leaning on the leather-covered vaulting horse, smoking a cigarette while C.S.M. Ross was making a few tentative strokes in the air with a thick shiny cane some four feet long. Over by the far window the B.S.M. was staring out into the soft summer evening, his back turned to the long bare room which emanated its usual smell of sweat, rubber shoes, and dust.

Cole stamped, saluted, said, "Sir!" to that distant back, received a brief nod, and then, relaxing into informality, strolled over to Calderon, pulling out cigarettes and matches of his own. "You here, too, eh? Picked for your looks or your strength?"

"Both, chum, I expect, like you," Calderon rejoined placidly. He shifted his six feet, three inches and uncrossed his legs. "F—ck! I gone an' creased me f—cking trousers!"

"Well, so long as you don't piss 'em, that's the main thing, i'nt it?"

"Don't see either of *us* has any call to do that. *He* may, though."

"Won't be wearing any," remarked Sergeant-major Ross briefly. He cut at the horse and Calderon moved back.

"Steady on, Sa'rnt-major. That near got me! I ain't done nothing—nothing anyone knows about, anyway." He turned to Cole. "What made you volunteer for this job, chum?"

"Sa'rnt-major's orders."

"Indeed?" Calderon raised an eyebrow in mock surprise. "Same thing with me, it was. Funny, ain't it, the way you an' me goes on volunteering our services like?"

"Duty," said Cole, his eyes slewed to Ross. "My King an' my country calls for volunteers. I take one involuntary step forward 'cos the Sar'nt-major's just given me a sharp shove in the back—simple as that. Not but what I *would* have volunteered if it had been Hood." Calderon gave an appreciative grunt of laughter.

Ross said warningly, "Sa'rnt Cole!"

"Sorry, sir."

"You're both volunteers; got to be. You knows that, and you knows why—'cos you're not in his company. Can't have any possibility of personal malice. Not that it would be likely, seeing as we only drills 'em, and his drill's not bad—now."

"Bloody frightful when he came."

"'Course it was!" Calderon grunted. "Poor little sod never seen a rifle 'fore he come here. Watching him the other day, I was. Picked it all up well enough now. Trouble is the Staff Major's always hanging around him—makes him nervous."

"Make anyone nervous, that would—like being watched by Frankenstein."

"Sa'rnt Cole!"

"Sorry, sir."

Sergeant Calderon asked curiously, "Sa'rnt-major, what's he supposed to have done? I mean, when I was told off—sorry—I mean when I volunteered for this

55

caper you could have knocked me down with a feather duster. Cane a cadet! *Jesus wept!* I thought. What's the management up to now? I mean to say, punishment drill's one thing, even Assault Course. An' talking of that, he was given a proper dose of that last week, if I remember right. Captain Lutwyche did it; Staff Major told him to, though. I heard him. 'Put Van der Haar over again,' he says. 'Been over twice, sir,' says Lutwyche. Staff Major just give him a look. 'Put him through the dannert tunnel, anyway.' Likes the dannert tunnel, the Major does."

" 'Cos of the blood."

"Kid comes out smothered in it. What'd you expect with Lutwyche shouting, 'Faster! Faster!' and running along beside? Staff Major called him up when he got out the other end, too. 'Stand still. Keep your head up. Look *over* my head, not *at* me.' Not easy, seeing the difference in their size. Told him off cold and slow, like he does. Then said, 'All right, go to the M.I. room and get iodine put on those cuts.' Kindhearted man, the Staff Major. Always got the men's welfare in mind."

"Did he go to the M.I. room to see it done?"

" 'Far as I can remember," said Sergeant Calderon carefully, his eyes on Ross's back, "he resisted that very powerful temptation."

Suddenly, B.S.M. Ulick swung around from the window and strode across to the waiting group. "Right! Smokes out! And no more silly talk from you, Calderon. It's none of your business why this is being done. As far as you're both concerned, it's management's orders; that's all there is to it. You're here to obey orders, and you'll obey 'em—got it?"

"Sir!" The two sergeants snapped to attention, their faces at once assuming the correct wooden rigidity of military subservience.

The evening light was fading quickly outside the windows. Ulick strode across to the complex of light switches on one wall and selected four. These were the floods of the boxing ring, and as they came on—four low-slung powerful lamps in great metal reflectors—pouring a glare of hot, vivid white light down on the vaulting horse and the men who stood around it. The B.S.M.'s brusque movement had knocked down another small switch in passing, and now a shaded lamp on the opposite wall, a lamp originally intended to light a dart board, illuminated in a golden glow a picture of King George in the scarlet full dress of the Grenadier Guards.

Mr. Ulick came back, his heavy boots stamping hollowly over the bare planking. "Now, remember what I've said, all of you. Ross, you take your . . ." He stopped abruptly and swung round as the door opened quietly at the far end of the room and shut again. No one spoke as Van der Haar slowly crossed the long shadowy room and uncertainly entered the pool of bright light. He was wearing nothing but his belted shorts of incorrect American beige drill and his rubber-soled gym shoes. Ulick suddenly remembered that, of course, in Egypt, unlike England, this was P.T. order. For a long moment there was silence while the four big men, embarrassed, unhappy, glanced awkwardly at the small, dark-haired, olive-skinned boy in front of them. His own large, fear-filled eyes slid quickly, furtively across their faces, and then rested, fascinated, upon the headless bulk of the shabby, leather-topped vaulting horse.

Ulick glanced quickly at Ross and saw that the Sergeant-major was concealing the heavy cane behind his trouser leg, while his other hand pulled nervously at his short brown mustache; nor were the expressions on the faces of Cole and Calderon such as to give the

B.S.M. any satisfaction. Both were beginning to look angry with that peculiar, sullen, smoldering rebellious anger of the British lower ranks.

Ulick let out his breath in a sharp hiss. "Right. Well now, we'll just run through this business quickly, see? So's we all know exactly what to do." He glanced at his watch. "The officers'll be here in a few minutes an' when they comes, we don't want no unnecessary hanging about. If we act lively an' don't make mistakes we can have them out of here in less'n eight minutes after they comes in, I reckon." He beckoned to Van der Haar. "Come over here. Now you stands here, see? Between Sa'rnt Cole and Sa'rnt Calderon—you two get into place."

The two tall Guards sergeants moved into position on each side of Van der Haar, dwarfing him by their uniformed bulk. Ulick moved back and, avoiding the boy's eyes, said, "Right. Now, when I tells you, you drops your trousers and comes over here. No, no, we'll take that for granted this time," for Van der Haar's hands had moved slowly, clumsily to the bright brass clasp of his white belt. "Now, come on—Sa'rnt Cole and Sa'rnt Calderon on each side; that's it."

They stood before the horse, and it was plainly much too high, its top level with the small brown nipples on Van der Haar's chest. "Got to lower the horse right down."

But even when the pegs had been pulled out and the wooden legs sunk as far as they would go into the interior of the horse, it was still too high. "No go," grunted Ross. Ulick nodded. "We'll have to have him on a box then. Cole! Get a box from the games room and jump to it! We haven't got so much time left."

The box at the foot of the horse put the matter right. Van der Haar mounted it and Ulick put a hand between his shoulders and pressed him down so that

58

he lay full stretch upon the smooth worn leather. "Now, your arms in front—that's it."

Everyone was in position. Ulick silently nodded to Ross to take his stance and measure his distance, and while the Company Sergeant-major was doing this he walked to the front of the horse and took something from his pocket. "Open your mouth."

Van der Haar lifted his face slightly from the shiny leather, glancing up uncertainly.

"Open your mouth a bit. No, no, you've no call to get scared." The B.S.M. showed a curved black piece of rubber cut from the wall of a motor tire and thickly wadded with cotton wool. "We don't want no noise, see? That's what this is for. Watch me, Cole. You're going to have to do this." He pushed the gag into Van der Haar's mouth and held it there, his hand spread around the boy's jaw. "You'll have to hold it in and keep his mouth closed. Your hands is big enough, that's why I chose you. Only, for Christ's sake, remember not to block his nose; he's got to breathe. Calderon, you'll be up by his head, too, so that the officers can't see this particular caper, which isn't in the book." He took the gag from Van der Haar's mouth and handed it to Cole. "Keep it in your pocket and get it back there afterward."

Cole suddenly said in a voice which Ulick had never heard before, "I don't like this! There's something gone f—ing wrong, I reckon! I didn't join the f—ing Army to do nothing like this. I'm minded to walk out—now."

Ulick saw at once that Cole had moved beyond the point at which discipline would control him. He wished he had chosen someone else, but it was too late now. He said bleakly, nodding down at Van der Haar, "I got you in 'cos I thought it likely you'd want to help *him*. 'Course, if you walks out now we'll have to send for someone else, an' the officers'll be here an' it will take about three times as long an' there won't be no way of shutting his noise, an' it will be just a shambles."

Cole swallowed. "All right, sir," he said.

"Then, for Chrissake, let's act sensible. When it's done, you get him on his feet and back where he was and get his shorts on. Don't worry about the buttons; get the belt fixed. If he's wobbly you holds him. Then I'll get rid of the officers, see?"

"Yessir," said Cole and Calderon almost simultaneously.

"Right. Then get back to your places and stand easy."

For a moment they stood there, the five of them, under the flood of white light; the half-naked boy between the two big immaculate Sergeants, and with the two senior N.C.O.'s a little to one side. And now there was only one more thing which Ulick had to say. He caught Ross's eye and beckoned him forward, then turned to Van der Haar. For a moment, an astonishing moment to all of them, he dropped entirely the hard brisk military manner with which daily, weekly, monthly he stamped through his duties at the training school. Putting a hand on Van der Haar's shoulder, he said gently, "Look, Michael, you knows Mr. Ross an' you knows—or should do—as he's got nothing against you. He's never done you no harm an' he doesn't want to now. Matter of fact, he asked me most particular to excuse him this duty, but I couldn't." Beside him, Ross nodded embarrassed confirmation. "Better show it to him, Ross."

Van der Haar looked silently at the heavy, shiny cane.

"Now, it's no use me telling the C.S.M. to go easy with this, see? Chances are you thinks I could do that, or perhaps that I already have. I can't, an' I'll tell you for why. If it's seen he isn't using his proper strength he can be told to do it again, see? An' with the Staff Major here, he would be. So instead of twelve you might get fourteen or fifteen, or even the whole lot over again. Understood? Good. Then just you think about what I told you this morning." He glanced at his watch. "Right. They'll be here any minute now." He moved three paces forward; Ross took three paces to the side; they both turned about, facing the door through which the officers would come, and a sudden silence fell over the big echoing room, dark and shadowy outside the one hot pool of central radiance and the single shining picture of the smiling King.

*I*N THAT silence—tense, ominous, expectant— Van der Haar stood motionless. His breathing was quick and shallow, his heart thudding rapidly, unsteadily. He was floundering in a terrified nightmare, running blindly through caverns of jumbled horror in which nothing made sense any longer. It was entirely unbelievable that this was happening to him; it couldn't be happening, but it was.

Throughout the long, hot afternoon he had wandered about the obscurer parts of the rambling old barracks, trying, with increasing incoherence, to discover what he had done to bring this thing upon himself and, still more vainly, how to deal with it.

He had been educated in the clear, rational lucidity of a French *lycée*, and the habit of logical, analytical thought had been deeply instilled into him. But instead of helping him now, this civilized accomplishment merely made confusion worse confounded. For he was in the hands of people—people who in everything except the accident of birth were foreigners—who had received a no less carefully instilled education of a radically different sort; an education that was in no sense logical or lucid, but which was based on national myths and a complex conspiracy of prearranged attitudes, an education that rated unconditional and enthusiastic conformity to a wide variety of beliefs and behavior patterns high above all other achievements.

Van der Haar had entered the training school in the belief that he was "to learn about the Army." He had expected textbooks, tables, diagrams illustrating the whole organizational complex, many hours of calm study interspersed with technical lectures. Instead, he had been made to run through barbed-wire tunnels and to smash his hands endlessly on the wood and steel of his rifle. He did not understand that the barbed-wire-tunnel running and the rifle drill were not inflicted on him to teach him about barbed-wire and rifles; they were part of a purposely painful and long drawn out initiation ceremony, and their purpose was moral and spiritual rather than physical. He did not understand that it was demanded of him that he show cheerfulness, willingness, and respect during this initiation, and therefore he too often showed his true feelings: despair, incomprehension, fear. These training methods were supposed to have a marked, permanent, and quickly discernible effect upon the outlook and attitudes of those undergoing them. But, since they were based on traditional instincts rather than explicable reasons, they could not be explained to Van der Haar in words, and so had no effect upon him. It was because of this that the officers said that he "behaved like a civilian"; his mind was not being reshaped in the correct way.

Hood, in Van der Haar's position, would have understood this. He would have realized instinctively that a refusal to conform mentally—though, in fact, Van der Haar was not refusing; he just did not understand what was required of him—was a sin against the whole glittering, towering structure of which the British Army was one of the main parts and its officers the most trusted custodians. Such a refusal implicitly demonstrated a lack of faith which could not be tolerated in anyone wearing a military uniform, for it was an impiety against everything that made up the creed of the British Army—Crown, Empire, Aristocratic-hierarchical rule, the Englishman's God-given right to trample on all foreigners or persons weaker or poorer than himself. It was a sin which merited very severe punishment indeed.

Also, it would have been apparent to Hood—being an Englishman in the full, rather than in the merely legal, sense—that he stood in a particularly vulnerable age group, neither child nor man; the time at which disbelief must be eradicated and the myths rammed home finally and, if necessarily, brutally and at whatever cost in suffering, so that they might become a part of the grown man to be perpetuated in him and enforced in turn by him in the years ahead.

Since Van der Haar knew none of this, he was at last forced to accept two facts stated plainly earlier in the day by Mr. Ulick. The officers wanted to do this to him and they were doing it because he was a boy, not a man. It made an odd sort of sense in a way, but it was a way Van der Haar preferred not to think about; somehow it brought back a shuddering remembrance of that night in the desert and Lutwyche's cold, exploring hand.

So then there remained the greater question of what he himself should do. Dollond. If only he could contact Dollond! But that, as he saw at once, was almost impossible. Dollond was in Syria and he might be in any part of the country, or even on leave. It would mean a network of complicated phone calls over military telephones, endless complex explanations, and almost certain failure. Anyway, as a cadet he would not be allowed to use the military telephone system without a permit from an officer, and even if he got out of the barracks, which at that hour was forbidden, he had not the money for a long-distance call on the still more difficult civilian lines.

Then there was escape. He could climb over the railings behind the ammunition store and drop down into the road beside the Museum of Antiquities that flanked the training school on one side. But he had been made to send his civilian clothes home—no soldier might be in possession of such things—and his passport and papers had been taken from him to be replaced with the regulation Army pay book. Also, since both Egypt and Syria swarmed with military police, let alone field security men in plain clothes, he would almost certainly be picked up before he got to the border. Even if by fantastic luck he reached home and his parents tried to hide him, the M.P.'s would get him in the end. And then—Lutwyche's words came back to him: "I don't think you'd like being an ordinary private in a line regiment for the rest of the war—or until you were killed—whichever is the shorter as the lawyers say."

So in the end the choice was narrowed to using his rifle bullet or letting events take their course. Van der Haar found himself wishing profoundly that the two things were the same, that this morning Ulick had been explaining a simpler ritual in which his part was merely to stand before a wall and await a single eliminating volley. It would have been easier to accept than the degrading horror which the officers had planned for him. But no one had suggested shooting him and, now that it came to the point, he saw clearly enough that a single bullet and a cumbersome Army rifle were by no means the best instruments with which to commit certain suicide; he would probably succeed only in blinding or maiming himself for life.

At that point his thoughts had come to a dead stop. He could neither escape his fate nor accept it, and his five-hour Gethsemane had been fruitless; he was not, after all, thirty-three years old and convinced of a divine mission; he was seventeen, in many ways young for his age, and very frightened.

And now he stood waiting between the Sergeants, feeling the arc lamps beating down on his bare shoulders while the sweat pricked out over his skin and dripped from his armpits and down the backs of his legs. He was acutely conscious of his body and what was about to be done to it, every nerve vibrant with feeling, every muscle pulsing with blood as his adrenal glands boosted them with the extra speed and strength for an escape that was impossible. For a moment he hung his head, panting like a horse, and in that moment there came from outside the sound of curt voices and footsteps; the door at the other end of the long room was thrown open, and B.S.M. Ulick bellowed, "Parade, parade, shun!"

*T*HE OFFICERS entered the gym in a close group led by Major Seligman, behind whom came the Staff Major, Lutwyche, and Hood. They were, with the exception of Exelfield, who still wore his boots and breeches and carried his eternal riding crop, dressed for evening mess; their pale tunics glinting with polished buttons and regimental insignia. They strode across the floor, their footsteps drumming loudly on the hollow planks, and entered the square pond of light with its five stiff, silent figures beside the low horizontal bulk of the vaulting horse.

Ulick saluted, snapped, "All present and correct, sir." And Seligman saluted in his turn. He was looking grimly, coldly angry, and his looks matched his feelings. It was only at lunch today that he had heard, at first with incredulity, later with rage, that Lutwyche had actually put Exelfield's atrocious plan to the test and had received official approval from the Colonel Commandant. He had sought the Colonel as soon as possible and protested vehemently. "Sir, it's not as if this was the peacetime Regular Army, or as if this cadet was a peacetime boy recruit! It's not even as if he'd committed any serious act of indiscipline, either. In fact, I understand that the charge brought against him was merely that of having an untidy locker. . . ." He had expostulated for several minutes, while the Colonel smiled at him kindly and waited politely for his turn.

When it came, he was as suavely calm and reasonable as ever. "My dear Seligman, I do indeed fully comprehend the points you've raised. What is more, I understand your feelings over this matter and I think they do you credit. Of course, you are quite right when you say that this is not the peacetime Regular Army and that this cadet is not an ordinary peacetime boy recruit and that the last charge on his crime sheet— taken by itself—is of a fairly unimportant nature. But the fact is—will you smoke; no?—the fact is, as I was saying, that these points you have raised are completely irrelevant to the present case. They have nothing to do with it at all. Perhaps"—he had sat back and examined the tip of his cigarette for a moment—"perhaps it would be easier to explain what I mean—and I assure you, my dear Seligman, that I am most anxious to explain my meaning to you—if I were to make a few points myself. Let me try to do so.

"Firstly, then, this establishment exists to train regimental officers and, as you know, we are supposed in some ways to run it on Sandhurst lines. Secondly, this cadet has been behaving, or perhaps it would be best to say *not behaving,* in a way that would be tolerated long at Sandhurst. There, a general charge of consistently unsatisfactory behavior would be quite enough to have him beaten; and the beatings, I may say, would go on until he adapted himself to the correct pattern. Now you may say, and I would emphatically agree with you, that this boy should never have been sent here in the first place. If Intelligence wanted him, they should have waited until he was the right age and then got him commissioned along with all the other odds and bods on the General Service List. Instead of which, some person or persons unknown decided to send him here, and from here he has, as you are well aware, to be commissioned into a proper regiment. When he leaves us it will be as an officer of a line regiment: Devons, Dorsets, Buffs, or some other. We know, of course, that he'll never actually serve with them; he'll be seconded at once to Intelligence. But he'll be on their official strength; he'll be wearing their badges and buttons, and that regiment will be *his* regiment.

"Well then, to put the matter bluntly, I want to think, for the sake of that regiment whose badges he will wear, that when he leaves here he will be a lot more like a regimental soldier—like an officer—than he is at present. I don't mind a twopenny damn what sort of fellow wears the General Service badge, but I *do* mind, very much indeed, about the type of officer who wears a regimental one."

"Van der Haar doesn't understand that point, sir. And I think you'll agree that it is one that a Regular soldier would be more likely to appreciate. Van der Haar doesn't know the first thing about the regimental system. I remember a paper exercise when he failed to use an entire company of Sherwood Foresters—he said afterward that he thought they were game wardens— and up till quite recently he apparently believed the Pioneer Corps to be some sort of shock troops." That had been a mistake; the Colonel's mouth had thinned at once.

"Yes, yes, most amusing, Seligman. The fact is that this young man makes a habit of such amusing remarks. I rather think we should break him of it. I've no doubt that he has no particular interest in becoming a regimental officer, in any case; he's merely interested in this job the Intelligence have waiting for him. Not, Seligman, a very commendable attitude in a young Englishman at this time, do you think?"

"He's—well, in many ways he's not really very English, sir. I mean, that's partly why Intelligence . . . ."

Gently, the Colonel had said, "As far as we here are concerned he *is* English, and he *is* going to become a junior officer in an English line regiment. Whether he likes it or not, we are going to try to fit him to the pattern suitable to both those positions. If a caning will help—and personally, from all I have heard about him, I believe it can do nothing but good—then he is still quite young enough to undergo one."

"This is to be a rather special kind of caning, sir."

"And, am I not right, Van der Haar has been sent here for special reasons. Like unto like, as they say." The Colonel had risen and laid a gentle hand on Seligman's arm. "I'm sorry to seem frivolous on a subject you seem to take seriously, my dear man. I assure you I'm not a bit, really. This will do that boy a lot of good; if I did not think so I would not sanction it. It will be, as I told Lutwyche this morning, a significant experience for him."

And at that point Seligman had realized that further protest was useless. He was up against a high, blank, and solid wall of irrational class prejudice and caste totems, a wall which guarded and shut from the defiling touch of ordinary men a mass of ancient privileges, rites, and traditions, a huge herd of ornamental but otherwise utterly useless sacred cows. By the Colonel's own admission, the sole reason that Van der Haar was to be punished—and in a particularly unpleasant way—was because the few square centimeters of embossed metal which he would have to wear on his cap and collar when he left the school were of a different design than the other few square centimeters of embossed metal he would have worn if it had been possible to commission him on the General Service List. Against such reasoning, if one could call it that, there was no argument at all.

Later that afternoon Seligman had received a polite note on the Colonel's own blue notepaper and written in the Colonel's own ornate hand requesting him to be present at the punishment parade that evening. The Colonel, "after due reflection," had decided that a second officer of field rank should be present, and as Major Seligman had shown an interest in the case it appeared that his would be the most suitable appointment.

Seligman had sat back marveling at the mind of the British Regular officer; it partook, he saw, of many of the qualities of the professional criminal. On the surface it was so stupid, arrogant, vain, and brutal that it appeared to the outsider to be vulnerable to any intelligent attack. But underneath that exterior lurked a thin, hard streak of infinite cunning which evaded and avoided the traps laid for it by those who looked only on the outward appearance. The Staff Major, Lutwyche, and young Hood were Regulars; he, Seligman, despite his official seniority, held only a wartime commission. If he was present this evening and if, in some way, this business backfired, he, as the senior officer, would carry the responsibility, thus shielding the others. It had happened before, of course; it was happening all the time. He had fought in three battles against the enemy and had been wounded in the last, whereas neither Exelfield, Lutwyche, nor Hood had ever been in action. The Regular Army looked after its own.

And now here he was, sullenly, darkly angry, at the head of three officers with whom, from a social viewpoint, he was hardly any longer on speaking terms; and Ulick was saluting with a look of surprise and indignation in his eyes, as if Seligman was the last person he would have expected to present himself as a witness this evening. Returning the salute, Seligman realized that this was something which must be put right later, for his relations with the B.S.M. had always been excellent. He glanced across at the figures on the other side of the white pool of light, and caught his breath sharply. This was going to be worse, much worse, than he had expected.

Van der Haar, in only his shorts and with a curving streak of dark hair fallen forward across his forehead, looked about fifteen at the most. He was obviously terrified, and it was almost possible to see his heart pounding under the rapid expansion and contraction of his chest. And now Seligman saw with a shock of mingled revulsion and pity that the damp skin of chest, shoulders, and arms was marked with small, newly healed red cuts; and he thought of the dannert tunnel, the long roll of circular strands of barbed wire through which the cadets were made to run crouching during the Assault Course. Somewhere he had read that before the more terrible of French medieval executions, the victims were *taillé*, ripped with iron hooks, to give them a foretaste of the agonies in store; and this, too, had not apparently been neglected tonight.

With the exception of his breathing, Van der Haar was managing to stand still; it was the one thing which weeks of shouting on the parade ground had made automatic; in the presence of officers one froze into an immutable, trancelike rigidity. His eyes alone, dark pools reflecting blank empty fear, moved rapidly across the faces of his tormentors opposite. And as for a second they met Seligman's, the Major thought he read one last, mute, despairing appeal for help. In that second he came within a hair's-breadth of calling the whole thing off. He even took one half-pace forward in order to do so. Then, abruptly, coldly, reason reasserted itself. If, by right of his rank, he dismissed the parade there would be an inquiry, and the matter would inevitably move up into the aloof regions of higher authority beyond the gates of the training school; and in that ambience of gilt and family connections, the Colonel, using all his influence as a Regular officer and a Guards officer at that, would thwart the Intelligence Corps' demand for their protégé and get Van der Haar posted as a private to an infantry regiment. After this morning's interview Seligman had no doubt at all about that. "You poor little sod!" he thought bitterly. "They've got you, all right. And they've got me as well; they've got us both." And then he was filled with a sudden sense of shame at trying to ease his conscience by coupling himself with Van der Haar, even in a passing thought. For what had he, who stood here washed and brushed in a smart uniform and who in less than half an hour would be drinking gin and lime on a jasmine-hung terrace under the calm evening sky,—what had he in common with that small, scarred, panting, sweating figure standing there mutely awaiting torture. For that, he told himself harshly, was what he and Exelfield, Lutwyche and Hood were here to see done; that, in cold dictionary terminology, was the word for it; that, and no other. They had trapped a small, harmless, and totally defenceless animal, and now they were going to torture it deliberately, wantonly, and with elaborate ceremony.

He shuddered and became aware that Lutwyche, as company commander, was reading the sentence: ". . . twelve strokes of the cane." His voice seemed higher than usual; was it excitement or fear or a mixture of both?

As soon as the words were out Ulick repeated them and swung round to Seligman. "Carry on, sir?"

Hardly moving his lips, the Major said tonelessly, "Yes, please, Sergeant-major."

Ulick saluted, swung round on his heel, and nodded briefly to Van der Haar. For a second the boy stood motionless under the huge white glare of light; then a sighing shudder seemed to pass over his whole body, his scarred, sunburnt hands lifted slowly to his childishly thin waist and fumbled with the glittering clasp of his Army belt. It came apart with a metallic click and hung heavily, and after he had opened the first three buttons of his shorts that weight brought them falling of their own accord past his narrow hips to his ankles. He stepped out of the crumpled circle of beige drill and stood completely naked, his eyes lowered, his face a dull burning crimson, before them all.

72

And Seligman understood at once that for Van der Haar this was perhaps almost the worst part of what they were doing to him. For, after all, he was a boy, not a man; that dark-skinned body with the slick, flat angles of male youth was completely hairless save for the small triangle at the base of his flat belly. He did not consider himself physically one with them, and had all the diffidence of a boy who knows his body is still growing, still maturing, not complete or solid. It could not have been much worse for him if he had been a girl.

Seligman slid his eyes to Lutwyche and saw, as he had half-expected, that the Captain's face was slightly flushed, his eyes behind the horn-rimmed spectacles gleaming with avid fascination. Seligman had long guessed the truth about Lutwyche, and now he wondered momentarily whether Lutwyche could possibly have made some sort of attempt at Van der Haar. But no, Lutwyche was not a fool; he would not risk his whole career in that way. It was probably largely because of Lutwyche's frustrated feelings that they were all here this evening.

And now, Van der Haar appeared to have become rooted to the floor. Lost in a sick morass of misery and humiliation he seemed to have forgotten that this was merely, as far as his official punishment was concerned, the unimportant prelude. Seligman saw Ulick motion quickly to the two sergeants, who had automatically taken a pace forward with Van der Haar when he stepped out of his crumpled shorts. Now they each laid a hand on his arms and led him the three steps to the box below the vaulting horse. Van der Haar moved slowly, head hanging, eyes dropped; he stumbled over the box, mounted it, and more or less fell face down across the long leather top of the horse. The two sergeants pulled his arms straight out in front of him while Ulick moved up, making some correction in a low undertone, and then turned to Ross.

And now, thought Seligman, we really get on the job. We're all back again in the eighteenth century and George the Third's at Windsor and everything's nice and elegant and cosy; scarlet regimentals, white wigs, and everyone in his proper place—us at the top and the rest well down beneath our feet. Nearly one-hundred-and-fifty years had passed since Waterloo, but to the Staff Major, Lutwyche, Hood—most of all to the Colonel—they had altered nothing important. The high walls of the barracks, the exclusive doorways of the officers' messes and clubs could keep out all but a vague murmur of the changing world; behind them it was possible to dream on in a daily round of regi- mental rites and ceremonies, rituals and attitudes as old as the regimental port and cognac with which the Royal toasts were drunk at dinner.

Ulick's voice shouting "One!" brought Major Selig- man back with a jerk from his second's escape into re- flective irony. He saw Ross take a sharp pace forward, saw the long cane swing flashing in a wide arc under the lights, and heard the sound that was neither a crack nor a thud but something of both as it struck Van der Haar's small taut buttocks.

Ross took a step back and lifted the cane once more while a long red welt sprang up, showing the site of the first stroke. It would be upon that thickening red line and on either side of it that Ross must lay the next eleven.

"Two!" shouted Ulick, and once more the cane came hissing down and struck with its odd sharp thud. This time Seligman's eyes were on Van der Haar, or as much of him as he could see behind Sergeant Calderon's broad back. He realized from the stance which Calderon had adopted beside the horse—legs

74

apart, shoulders braced—that both Sergeants were having to hold the boy down with all their strength. As the cane struck, the whole of Van der Haar's body jerked convulsively, and from the direction of his head, which was obscured by Calderon, came a queer half-stifled grunt.

"Three! Four! Five!"

Seligman felt something tickling his face and realized that he was dripping with sweat. His heart was pounding and he was feeling very sick. Van der Haar's thighs were now a crisscross of darkening crimson weals that stood out horribly under the electric glare from above. And still the heavy cane whistled down onto the tortured flesh.

It was now apparent to Seligman that the two Sergeants had the boy's mouth clamped in some way—probably they had a gag between his jaws—and that he was unable to breathe properly. For a dreadful second he pictured the terror of Van der Haar at this moment—held down in that iron grip, his body one blazing agony, his lungs bursting for the air that was being denied them.

"Six!" shouted Ulick's remorseless voice, and once more the small body stretched on the horse jerked under the stroke, but with a slower, less galvanic effort; he was weakening now.

An odd unreality seemed to fill Seligman. He started to shake his head, and the sweat drops spattered out and fell to the dusty floor. From three feet away, on his left side, Exelfield gave him a brief glance and then turned his gaze back to the horse. Seligman saw that Exelfield's face was as coldly calm as ever, his eyes as cool and certain; and in his high-peaked cap the silver death's-head badge glittered brilliantly in the light. He stood with his booted and spurred legs slightly apart, his hands holding his riding crop across the front of his breeches. There was nothing eighteenth century about Exelfield; his attitude, manner, stance were pure Dachau. Far away, in another land, scenes like this were acted out daily under other fierce electric lights before the cold-eyed gaze of men who also wore the *Totenkopf* in their caps; men who, Seligman now saw plainly, possessed exactly the same mentality as the Staff Major. There was no difference at all between them, save that when, in the not so distant future, Exelfield's foreign colleagues made their last brief, hopeless appearances before Military Tribunals or People's Courts, Exelfield would be back in England in full possession of his immense wealth, the rank, probably, of Lieutenant-colonel, and some half-dozen medals. The Staff Major's booted feet would still be clicking across some parade ground, while those of the others stood roped upon the gallows.

And now a cold darkness fell upon the Major that replaced all his former incredulous anger at hearing, this morning, what was to be done, and all his appalled horror at what, this evening, he was witnessing. An intelligent man and a realist, he had never accepted the more extravagant and self-deceptive boasts of his nation's statesmen and propagandists. In going to war, he had set out to defend what he knew to be a most imperfect society: hypocritical, unjust, drably mean-spirited. But he had also believed that it differed profoundly from the barbaric tyranny of the murderers and torturers to which it was now opposed. It was possible to read of the things that happened in the concentration camps and still to say with complete belief: "That couldn't happen here."

And yet, tonight, he, an officer of the regiment which had led the most famous, heroic, and useless cavalry charge in history, had allowed himself after one feeble protest to ape the squalid role of a German prison guard. Somewhere in the shadows the ghosts of the Light Brigade turned their elegant, cherry-colored backs.

"Seven! Eight! Nine! Ten!"

Every time the long cane struck, a cold hand seemed to clench itself into a fist in Seligman's stomach. He glanced at Lutwyche and saw that his face was pale, his eyes wide with a fascinated revulsion. Beyond him Hood's face was scarlet, his jaws set as grimly as if he himself was to be next on the horse. For a moment, the young Lieutentant's eyes, guilty and ashamed, met the Major's and then dropped quickly. Hood had temporarily been jolted out of his identity as a Guards officer into the reality of existence, in which he was, after all, still largely a boy himself. What was being done to Van der Haar was, in a measure, being done to him, too, for they were both of the same generation and must live together in the same world for much the same span of years. Hood wanted to get behind the great curtain wall of the barracks and dream away his life in the company of men like the Colonel, but to do that he must, like a monk, renounce realism and the outside world, and he was still too young to be able to do this with certainty.

"Eleven! Twelve!"

And Ross, turning away, lifting a hand to wipe the perspiration from his face; the long stick, its work done now, hanging limp at his side.

For a single moment no one moved; everything was motionless, as in a tableau, under the harsh light. The very air seemed exhausted, burnt out, used up. From his place on the wall opposite the head of the horse George VI simpered in gold and scarlet.

The whole area of Van der Haar's narrow buttocks was one blue-red tumescent bruise; a small trickle of blood wriggled down his left thigh, mixed with the sweat under the back of his knee, and slid pale pink down the smooth brown calf. Then Cole and Calderon had him upright, their hands under his arms, and half-pulled, half-lifted him off the horse. He swayed for a moment, staring about him, drawing in huge rasping gulps of air; his face was livid, the color of dirty putty, his eyes glazed blankly with shock. Then he was back in his place, and while Calderon held him Cole pulled on his shorts and clamped the belt. Seligman watched with shame and a dreadful burning pity while the boy's shaking hands fumbled to do up the disregarded buttons. He looked away, and in doing so his eyes met those of Sergeant Cole and read plain murder in them—read such hatred that he could hardly prevent himself taking a step backward. Then Ulick, stiff as a poker, was saluting, saying something, snapping some request to dismiss.

Seligman nodded. "Yes, please, Sergeant-major," he said thickly. He guessed that Ulick wanted the officers to leave immediately, and it was a desire in which he shared to the full. Hardly bothering to return the B.S.M.'s salute, he turned abruptly. "Come gentlemen," he grunted curtly, and, followed by the other three, strode away as quickly as his bad leg would permit—away from that square of brilliant light, across the echoing floor to the door and out into the night and the fresh air.

*I*T WAS past midnight when Major Seligman turned down the narrow street which led to the Museum of Antiquities and beyond it to the great looming bulk of the old barracks. He had drunk a great deal in the past five hours, but the bad whisky and worse gin had only heightened the feeling of dark unreality which had fallen upon him earlier in the evening, turning his anger and unhappiness into a muddled exasperation in which his thoughts strayed increasingly through streets of doubt into cul-de-sacs of blank unreason.

The four officers had left the gym in silence that evening, and in silence they had broken up. Lutwyche had walked rapidly off toward his quarters, while the Staff Major had strode away in the direction of the administrative office block. Only Hood had reluctantly accompanied the Hussar Major toward the officers' mess. As they turned down the graveled pathway between the storehouses and the vehicle park, Seligman had suddenly broken the silence to ask cruelly, "Well, did you enjoy yourself as much as you'd hoped?"

Hood, caught unprepared for such directness, had stammered something about "unpleasant duty" and "necessity for discipline," but Seligman was not in the mood to tolerate old-fashioned cant from someone as young as Hood.

"Christ! Don't try that line with me!" he had exclaimed roughly.

For a moment, Hood subsided into silence; then he said, almost placatingly it seemed, "You see, Lutwyche wanted it done."

They were under a lamp standard and Seligman turned on him at once. "We're not talking about *Captain* Lutwyche! And you seem to forget that you're speaking to a field officer."

"I'm sorry, sir."

"So I should hope," grunted Seligman, already a little irritated to find himself taking his exasperated anger out on such a dim-witted junior as Hood. Hood had behaved atrociously, of course, but only under the instigation and example of his company commander and Exelfield. More quietly, he said, "You haven't answered my question yet."

"What question, sir?"

"You know perfectly well. I asked whether you'd enjoyed yourself this evening."

"Of course, I didn't—sir!"

"Oh, for God's sake, Hood, cut that out!" said Seligman tiredly. "I'm not a fool. You wanted it done, didn't you?"

"No. I thought—that is—it seemed to me . . ."

"I heard you," said the Major patiently, "in the mess at lunchtime yesterday, shouting for Van der Harr to be caned. I want to know why. You say you didn't enjoy the actual performance, and I don't think you did . . ."

"I didn't! The Staff Major did."

"My God, Hood! We're not *discussing* the Staff Major! Well?"

"I've told you, sir." Hood's voice was sullen. "He needed disciplining. He behaved like a civilian. This will teach him."

"Teach him what, exactly? To love and admire the Army and to try to emulate its attitudes more successfully? Surely, even you, Hood, can't think that?"

Hood scowled and shrugged, shifting his feet in the gravel, and the Major sighed deeply. "Look, you know what we've done this evening, don't you? Not just you alone, I, too, and the others. We are all involved."

"I don't know what you mean."

"*I* think you do. Only you don't want to put it into words."

80

Hood stared down at his feet for a moment, then he burst out suddenly. "It was done to me, often! Not—not like that, I admit, but they hit me just as hard, harder, probably, because there weren't any officers watching. And it went on for more than a year!"

"And at school before that, I suppose?"

"Naturally. Didn't it happen to you?"

"I didn't go to one of those sort of schools, thank God. And I suppose you'll now tell me that it didn't do you any harm, that it was good for you."

"Probably both are true enough." Under the lamp's yellow rays Hood's young face looked positively mutinous.

Seligman drew a deep breath. "Don't you see, you little fool, . . ." he began. But then he looked at Hood and saw that it was useless. It was quite useless. Hood had been picked up as a child of eight or nine and thrown into the machine of organized English upper-class brutality, and he had emerged at twenty-three a perfect specimen: fit, strong, "manly," and with every bit of nonsense—all those feelings and emotions which made the whole difference between men and beasts and which the system so deplored—knocked completely out of him. The system had done a really first-class job on Hood; they should be proud of him. And, in fact, they probably were.

Seligman shook his head and Hood glared at him, hot-eyed. "Why are you laughing?"

"Oh, God, why indeed?" Controlling himself with an effort, Seligman tried to pat Hood's shoulder. He knew he had been horrible to Hood, trying to make him question things he had been taught never to question. But Hood shrank away and the Major said, "I'm laughing, as they say, in order that I may not weep. All right, Hood. You've told me what I wanted to know."

"Can I go now?"

"Go? Aren't you coming in to dinner?"

"I—I think I'll go out and have it in the town."

*T*HERE HAD been few officers in the mess that evening; practically all the younger ones seemed to have gone out to enjoy themselves in the city. A cherubic old quartermaster captain sat in a corner with his Siamese cat curled asleep on his knees, and four balding, middle-aged majors played tartly acrimonious bridge at a table on the terrace.

The Colonel Commandant, propped elegantly against the otherwise empty bar, read an air-mail edition of the *Times*. As Seligman came in, he folded this politely and smiled. "Good evening, Major. May I offer you something?"

Seligman gave a start; he had not noticed the Colonel's presence until too late to avoid it. "Oh, good evening, sir. Yes, thank you—a whisky if I may."

Yusef, behind the bar, heard the order and deftly supplied it, while the Colonel scribbled his initials on the small pad of slips. "And—how did it go?"

"What, sir?" asked Seligman.

"The business with that boy—what's his name—Van der Haar."

"It was done—as ordered," said Seligman briefly.

"I see, yes. It went off all right, then?"

Seligman said nothing. If you want all the gory details why don't you ask for them? he was thinking. Or better still, why didn't you come and watch, your-

82

self? Stand right up near the horse and get the full kick? Then you could go to bed tonight and dream about it as Exelfield will.

He waited, and the Colonel, twisting his glass by its stem between his long sensitive fingers, asked, "How did he take it?"

Seligman said, trying but failing to keep the disgust out of his voice, "He made no noise, if that's what you mean—poor little devil."

The Colonel gave the slightest of starts and his eyebrows lifted in mild deprecation. "I don't think we need be too sorry for him, Seligman. It will do him a lot of good. And, after all, he's still very young."

With lowered eyes Seligman in his turn swirled the liquor in his glass, but his hands were shaking with rage. He was thinking that, after all, there were certain things to be said for the dear, dead days of George the Third. A hundred-and-fifty years ago, for instance, he would have been able to throw the remains of his drink full in the Colonel's handsome eighteenth-century face, and follow it up two mornings later with a pistol ball in the Colonel's eighteenth-century heart.

A quick footstep sounded on the parquet floor and the Staff Major entered. He'd got himself out of his everlasting riding boots and put away his crop. "Good evening, sir."

"Hullo, Exelfield. You're a little late."

"Am I, sir?" Exelfield glanced at his flat gold wristwatch. "Yes, I suppose I am. I've been in the M.I. room, as a matter of fact." He caught Seligman's eye and gave a slight, mirthless smile. "Ross did a good job, very competent. Our young friend won't be able to sit down for at least a week, I'd say. Brandy and soda, Yusef, and don't forget the ice." He turned once more to Seligman, his thin smile glittering like the grins of the silver skulls on his collar, and as the light above the bar caught his eyes the Major had again the impression of looking through them into a dark, empty cavity.

Involuntarily, he gave a slight shudder and shifted his bar stool so that he was a little further from Exelfield. He realized suddenly that his normal antipathy for the Staff Major was based on sound instinct—based on fear. For he saw clearly that Exelfield possessed— or was possessd by—something that was fortunately very rare in human beings, a strong streak of genuine evil—dark, motionless, unadulterated. His conduct in the affair of Van der Haar had been actuated by an ugly cold-blooded cruelty, not by half-remorseful revenge for a wretched childhood and youth, as was the case with Hood; nor by guilty, feline pederasty, as with Lutwyche; nor by the insane reasoning of the Colonel Commandant. As far as the Staff Major was concerned, Van der Haar had merely been the best available victim. Later, there would be others. . . .

Finishing his whisky, Seligman asked curiously, "Did you rub in salt and pepper? That's the traditional culmination, isn't it?"

The Colonel looked both annoyed and shocked, but Exelfield only grinned; he knew what Seligman thought of him and the knowledge did not worry him in the least. "They put on iodine, that's all. Not that he could feel anything then, of course. He will later, though." There was a short pause. Exelfield continued. "He'll be stiff enough, I imagine. We'll loosen him up on the square tomorrow."

"But, will he be able to march properly? After the way Ross . . ."

"He'd better. I'll be watching him." Exelfield turned suddenly to the Colonel. "Another thing, sir, while I remember. May I see you privately sometime tomorrow about Captain Cross?"

"The doctor?"

"Yes, sir. He was in the M.I. room, of course. He was extremely insolent to me in front of this cadet and two medical orderlies. Ulick was there, too, and will corroborate what he said, if necessary. If Cross was not a doctor I should have placed him under arrest at once. As it is . . ."

"Very well, Exelfield; we'll discuss it tomorrow."

Seligman got up. "I think I'll have dinner out after all," he said abruptly. "I need a change from mess cooking. Oh, I nearly forgot." Turning back, he took a checkbook from his pocket, scribbled quickly, ripped out the completed check, and pushed it across the bar toward the Staff Major. "Here you are; buy yourself a rack or some thumbscrews or something."

But he had not eaten, merely gone from bar to bar drinking. There were a dozen difficult questions he wanted answered, questions which went far deeper than the reasons—which were not really reasons but emotions—that had motivated the Colonel, the Staff Major, Lutwyche, and Hood in their treatment of Van der Haar. With every newly filled glass that was set before him, he hoped, ever more despairingly, to struggle through a mist of doubt to at least one of those answers—and every drink seemed only to obscure them still further from discovery. What had occurred tonight had been a piece of military atavism, horrible by every standard of today, as incongruous, grotesque, macabre as it had been senseless and savage. Yet people, apparently civilized, educated people of a civilized nation, had wanted it done, conspired to have it done, and tried to justify it. Why? Was he, Seligman, the only one who could see clearly the implications behind that obscene little ceremoney of six hours ago? He had sighed and risen from the last bar, realizing that he had discovered nothing. He would go back now, and tomorrow and for the next month he would somehow have to protect Van der Haar, whom he had never liked personally—an odd little hybrid who had got himself, however innocently, into the wrong place at the wrong time—from further mistreatment at the hands of Exelfield and the others.

And at last he knew only that the world was very dark, far darker than even in his saddest moments he had ever conceived of it. For thirty-four years he had walked, often in sunlight, sometimes in shadow, but finding his own way forward without too much difficulty or sorrow, a man and therefore fallible in a man-made and therefore fallible world. But from to-night it was going to be different; he knew that. The darkness had crept closer; the track had narrowed ominously; and the rocks underfoot were sharp and heavy and cut his feet.

The moon was rising over the city as Seligman approached the Museum of Antiquities. The Museum was shut, of course; it was never, as far as Seligman was aware, opened at all. If anyone wanted to see the antiquities he must wait until after the war, a period which, at least, would have the effect of rendering them still more antique.

Turning the corner of the building, he heard a scuffle somewhere in the caverned gloom of the narrow street before him, a sharp cry of pain, the splintering crash of glass, and a laugh; then a heavy muffled thudding as of the beating of a carpet. He began running toward the sounds as fast as his limping left leg would permit, and at last, by the dim light of one of the sparse lampposts, he saw a crumpled figure on the ground and heard the running steps of the assailants fading in the dark emptiness beyond the lamp's rays. It would be a soldier, of course. Soldiers were always being beaten up and robbed in the midnight streets of the city, and as he panted up, his feet crushing broken glass, he saw, as he had expected, that the victim wore a khaki uniform. He pulled a flashlight from his pocket, but because of his heavy breathing and the shaking of his hand the beam did not at once fall upon the crumpled figure but beside it onto the dusty roadway. And there, right in the center of the spot of light, shone a pair of undamaged horn-rimmed spectacles—Lutwyche's spectacles.

Seligman thought afterward that had it not been for the spectacles he would have been a long time identifying the body, for there was nothing recognizable left of Lutwyche's face; a heavy bottle filled with sand had been smashed across it, and then, with the rest of his head, it had been kicked into a dreadful gory pulp. Quickly, Seligman bent and lifted the Captain's limp wrist, but even before his fumbling fingers found the stilled pulse he knew that Lutwyche was dead.

And now, rising to his feet, he began to swear; to swear furiously, incoherently, repetitively at Lutwyche, at Exelfield, the Colonel, Hood, Van der Haar—and at Sergeants Cole and Calderon who had done this. He knew that as well as if they had strolled back out of the darkness, the blood still wet on their heavy steel-tipped boots, and told him so. He not only knew that they had done it; he knew why; he had seen the look in Cole's eyes just before the officers left the gym. And before that Cole—and Calderon, too, probably —had seen the peculiar excited expression on Lutwyche's face just before they put Van der Haar over the horse; and they had understood what it meant. For, like most of the British working class, the two Sergeants would tolerate a large amount of savage brutality so long as there was no faintest suspicion of any sexual implication involved in it. As soon as that happened, or as soon as they were able to detect it, the strong puritan streak in their natures, the well-known English fear and hatred of sex in any but its most rigorously chaste forms, sent them berserk.

And they had done what they had decided must be done with typical speed and almost certainly a high degree of cunning. Lutwyche had probably been condemned before he had got back to his quarters from the gym; his trapping and death planned to the last detail before he had left the barracks an hour later. And the alibis the two Sergeants would have arranged for themselves would probably prove faultless, proof against all the suspicions and questions, the boards and the courts of enquiry, and the endless paper work which tonight would drag for weeks and months in its wake. And he, Seligman, would be deeply involved in all of it; he saw that plainly enough. His rage should have mounted at the thought, but instead it dwindled and died. After all, in a way he was responsible; he might easily have prevented it all from happening.

Standing over the still body in the roadway, his thoughts went back to a calm spring evening three months ago. He had been in his own office rather later than usual, he remembered now, discussing a last-minute change in "E" Company's training program with Lutwyche. A knock on the door, Staff Sergeant Haseltine saluting in the entrance, and behind him a small, weary, travel-stained figure in a cheap-looking civilian suit, carrying a fiber suitcase. They had called him in, examined the crumpled papers he was clutching in an envelope, and shaken their heads over the way the Intelligence Corps recruited its peculiar personnel. Seligman's leg had been hurting, he remembered, and he was tired with all the extra work which the commencement of a new course necessitated.

88

The first thing he had ever said to Van der Haar had been the routine inquiry every officer made when a soldier reported at the end of a journey, "Have you had anything to eat?"

"No."

"Say 'sir' when you speak to the officers," Haseltine had prompted gently.

"All right, Staff; he doesn't know yet. Will you take him away and see he gets some supper? Oh, and there's the question of his company, isn't there. Lutwyche, would you mind having him? It'll be rather a . . ."

"That's all right. We'll manage."

"Good. Thank you. Now, you—Van der Haar—this is Captain Lutwyche, your company commander. He will be in charge of you while you're here. If you're in any difficulty or want to know anything you can always come to him. You understand?"

Seligman, standing in the dark road, shook his head despairingly. Why had he done it? Surely, even then, he had known—guessed very strongly at any rate—about Lutwyche. If only he had said, "I won't trouble you with him, Lutwyche. He can go to 'B' Company" or " 'D' Company." But he had been tired and his leg had hurt, and Lutwyche had been present in the office.

For that matter, why couldn't Lutwyche have allowed his peculiar emotions a more normal outlet and lavished an affectionate favoritism upon the boy; in the circumstances, no one would have worried. Instead of which, through fear of discovery, vanity, and caste prejudice, he had twisted those emotions into a sanctimonious, smiling sadism.

Seligman looked down with a mixture of pity and disgust at the gory-headed thing huddled in the dust at his feet. "You poor bastard!" he said softly. "You poor, furtive, side-eyed fumbler! It's probably been coming to you for a long time, something like this. And now it's happened at last."

He should summon aid at once; he should run to the great arch of the barracks gate at the end of the next road and call the Guard. But there was no point in doing the first and he was curiously reluctant to do the second. He realized, with a sardonic acceptance, that he intended to do his best to shield Cole and Calderon from discovery. It was probably unnecessary, for they were capable of taking care of themselves; but there had been enough pain and blood and disaster without adding courts-martial and firing squads to tonight's work. He would say that he had seen Lutwyche's assailants and was certain that they had been Egyptians. He drew a deep breath of the still night air and leaving that ruined body in the dark shadow of the wall beside which it lay, limped slowly away through the moonlight down the road toward the guardhouse.

*T*HE RISING MOON washed one clifflike side of the great barracks with silver light, throwing shadows from the heavily barred windows into the long dark rooms behind. Shadow and cold white light fell across Van der Haar's sleeping face, where he lay on his bed in a corner of the barrackroom. He lay motionless, one arm thrown up as if for protection above his head, drugged with physical and mental exhaustion and a heavy dose of barbiturate. He was in no pain and had been in none for hours, for as soon as the Staff Major had left the M.I. room Dr. Cross had stabbed a needle into his left arm. By tomorrow morning the physical shock of what he had undergone would have largely worn off; but the spiritual one was a heavy, ugly scar he must carry for the rest of his days, learning patiently over the years how best to live with it and accommodate himself to it, allow for its irk and ache in all his changing moods, attitudes, and thoughts.

But now, for the next few hours of night and peace, he knew none of this. In the depths of sleep he dreamed of Beirut with its long, curving water front, gardens, squares, and fountains. He stood by the sea and the bright waves glittered in morning sunshine, and he was free again and happy and at home. He smiled slightly in his sleep, and the moon, rising still higher in the vast night sky, lifted the bars of shadow slowly from his face.

ABOUT THE AUTHOR

Gwyn Griffin has spent much of his life in Africa, where he was born. At seventeen he had already become a cotton planter in the Sudan; at eighteen he was in Abyssinia, working as cipher officer to Major (later General) Orde Wingate. He served with the Colonial troops from 1941 to 1945, and then was Superintendent of the Colonial Police.

Mr. Griffin has lived and traveled in the Middle East, England, Australia, Spain, and the Canary Islands, and now lives in Italy. He is the author of six novels: *The Occupying Power,* which was published only in England; *By the North Gate, Something of an Achievement, Master of This Vessel, Freedom Observed,* and now, *A Significant Experience*—all published by Holt, Rinehart and Winston.